Also by this author:

Dodging Shells

Table of Contents

Chapter 1

The Beginning

"In the beginning God created the heaven and the earth."

A project of this impressive scope might very well have involved a lot of heavy lifting so I suppose we are meant to assume that God was male. Well...maybe. We'll get back to that.

"And God said, Let there be light: and there was light."

That was a good move, because otherwise that whole heaven and earth thing might have gone completely to waste. In the dark, who would have noticed?

Here's our dilemma: we are to believe that God installed the lighting promptly and without a single soul there to nag him about it. Now, does that sound like a male to you?

Never mind. Let's just follow the action and see where it leads us.

"God saw the light, that it was good."

So God doubtless had a beer or whatever, and spent a few moments admiring his handiwork. That sounds about right.

"...and God divided the light from the darkness."

Now we have night and day following each other in a sensible and orderly progression and the first day's work is complete.

On the second day he divided the waters on the earth from the waters above the sky, which was to prove especially helpful for sailors. They would find it challenging enough worrying about sailing off the edge of the earth without the additional danger that they might at any moment drift off into the clouds and lose track of which way was up.

The third day was busier. God gathered together the waters into seas, allowing dry land to appear here and there. Then the earth was made to bring forth grass and herbs and trees and all fruit and veggie stuff. It was a big job and he required two breaks in order to adequately relish his achievement, but I think he must have bypassed the liquid refreshments this time, or so much would never have been accomplished in only one day.

On day four, God made the moon and the stars to light the night and the sun to light the day, and he cleverly made the sun brighter, so everyone would be able to tell when it was daytime. After yet another break to appreciate the results, we move on to day five.

He spent day five creating the creatures that live in the waters and the birds that fly in the skies. There were quite a lot of them so when he was done, he just took a quick admiring glance and called it a day.

On day six, well rested and bursting with energy, God created the many beasts of the earth. As diverse as they were, they seemed remarkably harmonious —rather beautiful, in fact—and doubtless got along well together, having no reason to quarrel. Then, perhaps in a playful attempt to stir things up a little, God fashioned man out of dust and gave him permission to boss everything around.

It's interesting to note that he included a labour-saving feature in each plant and fish and bird and beast and human. They were able to reproduce themselves, making it unnecessary for him to run through this creating stuff so often as to become boring. Every once in a while, God simply said "Be fruitful, and multiply", and they did. In fact, the humans made quite a big thing of it, not being perceptive enough to realize that God himself obviously found it a chore tedious enough to warrant automation.

Now, here's our first real clue to God's gender. On the seventh day, he considered the work finished, and he rested. After all the breaks taken to admire the work in progress, God still felt that he needed to rest on the seventh day. All day.

This evidence does seem to suggest that God was male. He clearly had no expectation of starting it all over again the next week. He figured he was done. A woman would have known better.

Having established that God was, in all probability, indeed male—at least at that time—we may attempt to draw some conclusions about his appearance. We're told that God aimed at creating man 'in his own image'. Do we assume, then, that he tricked man up to look exactly like him? Why would he do this...so the beasts would be fooled, allowing them all the more easily to be dominated by man? That would seem unnecessarily theatrical. Perhaps he didn't mean exactly like. Maybe just sort of like.

Well, in what ways like and in what ways sort of different? Men have made a great fuss over the years about their resemblance to God, feeling justified in considering themselves superior, for example, to women—who, clearly, look a lot different. But we have no proof that even the very first man was all that similar in appearance to God—let alone some of the really unattractive men who have come later—so it's rather foolish to make much of this point. Let's simply assume man looked more like God than, say, fish did and leave it at that.

Having created a pretty fine world, God then outdid himself by gathering together all the best bits, and creating a splendid garden in Eden for the man to tend. He saw that man—who even then was apparently not up to much—would need a companion to help him take care of the place, so while he was deciding what sort of creature would be most helpful, he hit on a project to keep man busy and out from under foot.

"I need you to name all the beasts and plants. It's a big project—very important. Take all the time you need." This turned out to be an excellent idea, because it made the names easier for man to remember, and God probably wrote them all down somewhere for his own reference.

By the time man had chosen a fitting name for everything (he chose the name Adam for himself) God had made his decision. He took one of Adam's ribs when he was asleep and wouldn't notice, and fashioned out of it a woman, Eve, to keep him company. Eve, who was sensitive to these little distinctions, did not fail to notice that she had been created from flesh whereas man had only been wadded together from a handful of common dust, but she didn't want to start a fight right away so, tactfully, she refrained from pointing that out.

In stocking the garden, the tree of the knowledge of good and evil had been planted in amongst all the others, without a moat or even a ditch to protect it. As soon as God noticed this oversight, he called Adam to his side.

"You see this tree? Well, I want you to keep away from it. Understand?"

"Yes...can I eat the fruit? The fruit looks good."

"No. I just finished telling you. Keep away from it."

"How about pears? Can I eat pears?"

"Yes, eat all the pears you want. Just keep away from *that* tree."

"Is it ok if I eat cherries?"

"Yes."

"How about..."

"Look," snapped God, "Eat whatever else you like. But if you eat the fruit from that tree—even a single bite—you'll be sure to die. You got that?"

Adam nodded mutely but God left wondering whether the concept of death had entirely penetrated that murky brain. He decided to try again later. Adam had already appeared to be developing a bit of a headache.

Neither of them had noticed the serpent, lounging in the grass, well within earshot. But the serpent, who was getting bored being the only smart beast in the garden and having no one at all intelligent to talk to, fancied he saw some potential in Eve. So he tempted her to sample the fruit of the forbidden tree before God decided to put up a fence or something.

"The apples are red and juicy, and so sweet," he coaxed. "They can't hurt you. Look...I'll eat one myself."...and he did. But his wits were sharp already, so it had no effect on him. He smacked his lips. "Mmmm...delicious. Have one."

"I don't think so," replied Eve, suspiciously. "There are plenty of other tasty looking fruits in the garden. If I get hungry, they'll do fine."

"Ok, ok. It's not about the flavour," he admitted, wondering if she wasn't already rather smarter than she looked. "These apples are from God's 'Special Stock'. Eat one and you'll begin to understand things. You'll find some answers, but more important...you'll start to know the right questions. It'll open the doors of your mind. What do you say?" This sounded a lot more interesting than just hanging around in the garden with Adam and the dumb beasts, so she gamely took a bite. She had overheard God's warning, of course, but she thought when he realized what clever company she had become, The Lord would change his mind and spare her life. No sooner had she swallowed the fruit than she began to notice how dumb Adam really was.

"You know, a little knowledge wouldn't do you any harm," she commented. "Why don't you try a bite?"

For his part, Adam didn't care much about getting smart (the serpent had known he would be a tougher sell), but the fruit looked yummy so he didn't put up a lot of resistance. After all, Eve had eaten it, and she still seemed healthy enough, so how dangerous could it be?

Now that they had gotten wise, it took Adam no time at all to notice they were also naked. And once it caught his attention, he noticed it constantly. Becoming uncomfortable with his persistent ogling, Eve invented a needle and devised a cunning way of sewing fig leaves together into aprons to cover their nudity in a fashion both modestly discreet and unpretentiously stylish. Unfortunately, when God saw Adam and Eve in their clever fig leaf pinafores, he knew they must have been eating the forbidden fruit, because they hadn't been nearly that smart when he had last encountered them. It might seem petty in retrospect, but The Lord was not prepared to share his reputation for wisdom with any neophytes. He was plenty angry. He questioned Adam, who immediately whined that Eve had tempted him (not very gallant, but there it is: the precedent was set, and man has been blaming woman for his transgressions ever since). Eve, taking her cue from her husband, blamed the serpent. And since the serpent was too clever for his own good, God didn't give him an opportunity to state his case, so we'll never know who he might have blamed if he'd had the chance. In a rage, God doomed the serpent to slither through the dust on his belly for the remainder of his miserable life, and guilty consciences on both sides ensured that humans and snakes would never again be really close pals.

To punish Eve for her disobedience, The Lord devised a creative (under other circumstances, we might even say diabolical) strategy. He infected her with carnal desire for her husband—she hadn't thought much of him up until then—and he arranged that the resulting childbirths would be both painful and dangerous.

"Wait." said Eve. "Let me be sure I understand this babies thing. These items are how big?" She was already beginning to learn the right questions.

"And they come out of *where?*"

In addition, Adam was henceforth allowed to rule over her. It's unclear whether God meant this particular punishment to be hereditary but men, never slow to seize an advantage, have argued ever since that it had been intended to apply to all women...and for all eternity.

Nevertheless, Adam would not go unpunished. "If you think you're going to continue hanging around here, just poking about with a rake a bit," said The Lord, "you're very much mistaken. From now on things won't be so easy. You're going to have to work up a sweat to earn your keep...or you'll have to watch someone else sweat..." He apparently considered this almost as bad, though man came to prefer it.

Adam and Eve were driven out of the garden, and angels were posted with flaming swords, to prevent their return. This might seem excessive but, you see, there had been a *second* magic tree in the centre of the garden: the tree of life. Now that Adam and Eve were beginning to think things out for themselves, The Lord wasn't keen on allowing them to sample the fruit of that tree and live forever, continually asking him a lot of irritating questions. And sensing in Adam a male ego comparable to his own, he was also not about to tolerate potential rivalry from an immortal upstart.

Perhaps it was just as well. Since he had equipped them to fruitfully multiply, it's clear that the earth would have become awfully crowded if humans had remained immortal: they would have been stacked up like cordwood in no time. But henceforth men and women would live their allotted years, then die and crumble back into the dust from which they had originally come: neat, efficient, and ecologically sound.

As a parting consolation gift, God presented Adam and Eve with fur coats.

Eve wondered: were her fig leaves getting brittle...maybe starting to curl in too revealing a manner at the edges? She glanced down nervously. Not yet.

"Thanks so much. They're lovely," she said, not wanting to appear ungracious. "But really...you shouldn't have."

"It was nothing," replied The Lord, modestly. "They're recycled materials."

"Oh, well, that's alright then. But wait..." she pondered, "how did they come off the previous owners? You didn't..."

But God had already thought of several other important things he needed to do, and was hurrying away.

Within the first couple of years after setting up housekeeping somewhere that wasn't in the garden, Eve bore two sons: Cain, who became a farmer, and Abel, who tended sheep. Because they were hard-working lads, crops were plentiful and the flocks thrived. In an attempt to honour The Lord for this bounty Cain approached the local altar with an offering of produce while Abel offered a lamb. God was apparently not a vegetarian, for he enthusiastically praised Abel's offering while showing no appreciation at all for Cain's gift. Eve, who had learned a lot about mothering as the boys grew up, could have warned him that this was bound to cause conflict between the brothers, but she hesitated to offer unsolicited advice and God was too busy anticipating the juicy flavour of roast leg of lamb to consider the effect of so insensitively revealing his obvious preference. Cain might well have sulked awhile then gotten over it, but as younger brothers will, Abel gloated openly over his success.

"Don't feel bad. Your stuff was nice too. But ...well...did you *smell* that roast lamb? You have to admit...

"Look," he continued, with smug all over his face, "I'd be glad to have a look before you offer the next batch...maybe suggest some more appetizing recipes, or perhaps a more attractive presentation. No...honestly

...it's no problem. I'm sure there's *something* we can do to make your gift as appealing as...well...mine."

Humiliated, Cain was overwhelmed by the need to lash out at someone and, as God would obviously be a bad choice, he lashed out at his brother until Abel was dead. To make matters worse, when The Lord subsequently asked about Abel's whereabouts, giving Cain an opportunity to admit his guilt and do some repentant grovelling, he casually replied, "How should I know? Am I my brother's keeper?" This was pretty cheeky under the circumstances, and only made him look bad. As punishment, God dramatically condemned him to wander as a fugitive and vagabond, cursed through all the earth.

"Through all the earth..." mused Cain, "That sounds awfully public. So it's not going to be just personal, like between you and me?"

The Lord assured him that he was planning to make the curse very public indeed. Everyone would know.

"Well..." complained Cain, "you may as well simply strike me dead now! How far do you think I'll get with that hanging over me? I mean...I didn't expect to win any popularity contests after that fratricide thing, but seriously! There'll be a world of folks out there figuring to make points with you by bumping me off. I won't last a week."

He had a point. So God branded his mark on Cain —someplace conspicuous, no doubt— and promised some most unpleasant consequences for anyone who tried to kill him. The Lord preferred that Cain should live long and suffer, and he didn't want anyone interfering to spoil his plan.

As soon as he could pack his things, Cain set out with his wife for the land of Nod, on the east of Eden. (Clearly, while Adam and Eve were the first man and woman, they were not the only ones, which was a lucky thing for the gene pool.) Mrs. Cain was apparently condemned to wander along with her husband, although she'd always warned Cain to control his temper. "I know your brother was an irritating little snot," she scolded, "but couldn't you simply have *told* him so? Did you have to go do something *stupid?"* Cain wasn't much of a talker—over the years it had made her a bit shrill.

Furthermore, because Cain had spilt the blood of Abel on the ground, it would no longer yield its crops to him. That left his wife to struggle with the farm work alone—for they still had to eat. "I'm so lucky to have you covering all the footloose, vagabonding stuff while I see that there's food on the table," she mocked. "I know it must be a *terrible* hardship for a guy..."

It *is* hard to see how this was fair, as she was the innocent one, but justice was not always The Lord's strong suit.

After a few years, when he figured that God might have lost interest in their punishment, Cain risked settling down and built a city. His overworked wife had a lot to do with that decision.

For the next several thousand years Eve's family, split as they were, devoted their attention to being fruitful and multiplying. By the time fruitful multiplication had been in effect for many centuries, man's flesh was warring with his spirit in some pretty unpleasant ways. The Lord saw the wickedness embodied in the men he'd created and decided that he had made a huge mistake. We're not told whether this applied to the women too, but when he decided to wipe the men out, the women got included—by proximity.

Having developed the fancy that men had infected the earth itself with their violence, God was determined to destroy the whole thing in a colossal flood.

Never hesitant to play favourites, he set his mind on saving the only man who appeared to be righteous—and came from the correct blood line. So he gave Noah, who was a direct descendent of Adam, exclusive and detailed instructions for building a really big boat and told him to get busy.

Noah perused the plans. "This is a really big boat," he commented.

"Yes...well..." muttered The Lord.

"Way too big for just me. I'm guessing you have something else in mind."

"Oh. Didn't I mention? I noticed your lovely wife and charming family. I knew you'd want to bring them along as well."

"Yes...of course. Thanks. Still...it's a really *big* boat."

"Well, there *is* something else you can do for me. I want you to round up two of every living creature on earth—one male and one female of each—and make room for them all on board. It'll save me the trouble of creating a whole new batch once this, um, unpleasantness is over."

"Hey...I don't know. That's a lot of creatures."

"Look, it's the best deal you're going to get. You've got other offers?"

Noah didn't see that he had a whole lot of options, so he agreed and he and his family were spared, along with a representative selection of fauna. The rest of humanity, of course, and any other living thing that couldn't fly or swim through forty days and forty nights of torrential rain were drowned in the resultant flood, which effectively covered the entire earth.

After five months, the water started slowly to dissipate and the vessel rested, stranded on Mount Ararat, but it was nearly six more months before the earth was dry enough for the family and their cargo of creatures to leave the boat. And don't think that Noah's wife and the wives of his sons weren't counting the days. Preparing tempting meals without a fire, as they were forced to keep the windows firmly closed throughout the pouring rain, had been a challenge, and only a fool would believe that the men lifted a finger to clear the mess those animals made all that time. They were much too busy playing at admiral and patting each other on the back for their outstanding righteousness.

They had barely stepped off the boat before God started encouraging them all, once again, to be fruitful and multiply. "The whole thing will probably just happen all over again," he grumbled. "But that flood has left an awful mess. I promise not to wipe out the whole works the next time. At least," he amended," I won't use quite so big a flood to do the job." He left himself a little leeway for other forms of mass destruction.

As a thoughtful touch, he created rainbows to symbolize his promise that he would never again send such a flood—and also, perhaps, as a gentle reminder that he could if he wanted to.

Just as before, God granted men dominion over all the other beasts. But there were a number of improvements he wanted to see.

"You are not to eat a living thing," he stated. "If the blood's still flowing, keep your teeth off it. I heard a rumour about a particularly odious parlour trick that was becoming popular before the flood. Some guys were tearing the heads off live chickens with their teeth. I don't know if it's true, but if it is, cut it out! It's a nasty habit, and it's not funny.

"And anyone who intentionally kills another person will have to be put to death. I know the punishment is severe, but I'll have to insist. However, I'll always be busy doing something else, so I'll let you do the dirty work."

Unfortunately, The Lord did not think to limit inebriation. Perhaps he assumed that tacking a hangover on at the end would do the trick. Clearly, he underestimated the determination of his audience. At the first available opportunity, Noah downed so much new wine that he collapsed, dead drunk, in his tent. His son Ham, entering innocently, nearly tripped over his father's intoxicated body sprawled stark naked on the floor. Overcome with confusion and embarrassment, he stumbled back out the door. The experience left him understandably shaken—after all, Noah was over six hundred years old at the time and well past his prime—so when he ran into his two brothers right outside the tent, discretion was not foremost in his mind. In a misguided attempt to purge the distasteful image from his memory, he blurted out his troubling discovery to what he thought would be sympathetic ears. Immediately Shem and Japheth, who were more self-righteous than righteous, scrambled to find the nearest suitable garment and, laying it awkwardly across their shoulders, pretentiously backed into the tent to cover their father's nakedness without risking defilement through even the most accidental glance. When Noah awoke, he took one look at the unfamiliar garment covering him and realized what a drunken sot he must have appeared. In his shame, he cast about for someone else to blame.

When he learned that Ham had been the one to view his humiliation, Noah chose him. "I understand you intruded on my privacy, and saw me in a rather...um...dishevelled state," he said, with as much hauteur as the situation would allow.

"Yes," Ham mumbled. He was still struggling to scour the memory from his brain cells. "It was a mistake. I left immediately."

"...and yet you thought it would be appropriate to broadcast the news? My god, can a man not get 'dishevelled' in his own tent without media coverage? You disgust me!"

In his rage at this betrayal, Noah decided to punish not Ham himself but Ham's son Canaan, who hadn't even been there at the time and had absolutely nothing at all to do with the issue. With wondrous male logic, he made Canaan a servant to his sanctimonious uncles in order to punish him for the embarrassment that his father had inadvertently caused. The injustice of this defies all reason. We can only wonder at Noah's inability to find a way to blame his wife for some part of his discomfort, as well. She must have been out of the country on some errand at the time.

This revealing episode gives us some insight into the lofty nature of the man God had chosen, above all others, to save. He must have been the best of a very bad lot, which would help to explain the drastic use of a weather condition of devastating proportions to eliminate all the other guys. The wonder is that Noah was spared at all.

When Noah's family grew large enough to build a city, a few of the men dreamt of constructing an impressive tower: one that would reach right up to heaven. "Ours would be bigger than everyone else's," they mused. "Much bigger. Think how jealous all the other cities would be...and we would be closer to God than all the rest. That should be worth something." But it would be a massive undertaking and those few despaired of ever being able to accomplish it. They got together over their wine, day after day, neglecting their chores as they complained that it would take them several hundred years, working full time, to accomplish their dream. By that time they'd be getting too old to enjoy it and the earliest bits would already be getting shabby.

Finally their wives got fed up with handling all the work the men should have been doing, so they discussed the problem amongst themselves and formulated a plan. Preparing a huge feast, they invited the whole family (which was a multitude by that time) and over the cooking fires they convinced their sisters, aunts and cousins to organize all their men. With everyone working together, the tower would be built in no time at all.

"So how's *that* going to help? Do you think they'll lift a finger to help around here as long as they have a *project?"*

"Yes, every time there's a seed to be planted or a roof to be mended it'll be: "I'll do it later...I have to get over to the tower...the guys need me."

"Just like now?"

"Well...yes."

"But it's bound to make a lot of extra work for us. They'll have us fetching and carrying and who knows what all, while they do all the fancy stuff. And they'll expect snacks *all* the time. And the dirty clothes! We'll end up doing a lot more than our share before this thing is done, you know."

"So what's new?"

"...true."

"But once it's built—once they have a bigger one than all the other guys—maybe they'll stop obsessing, and get back to doing some of the work around here."

"It'll never happen."

"You have a better idea?"

The plan worked: the tower was built and named Babel, the men felt really important every time they saw it (they looked at it a lot), and eventually they started to help with the chores again.

But they had seriously misjudged The Lord's reaction to the proximity of such intrusive neighbours. He considered heaven to be his special domain, and he wanted none of their great ugly towers poking up into his space. Furthermore, it was most unsettling to see what people could do when they cooperated. Each man separately was nothing much, but God worried that together they could accomplish wonders which might make his own miracles look somewhat less impressive. Thinking fast, he re-wired their brains so that they could no longer understand each other's speech. Never again would all of the people be able to work together on any one project and, within about a day and a half, enough misunderstandings had developed to ensure that their effectiveness as a species would henceforth be significantly impaired. Just for good measure, God then scattered them over the face of the earth—and they stayed scattered.

Chapter 2

The Chosen Ones

After the passing of many generations, God insisted that Abram, who was a distant descendant of Noah (no surprise...everybody was), pack up his wife and nephew and all their household goods and leave their home in Mesopotamia, promising that he would become great and powerful in a new homeland of The Lord's choosing. But the land of Canaan, which appeared to be The Lord's choice, was experiencing an unanticipated famine at that time, so Abram put his illustrious destiny on hold and continued on into Egypt, where he might feed his family.

Having way too much time to brood as he was trudging along, Abram became obsessed by the notion that the beauty of his wife Sarai was sure to attract the attention of some powerful Egyptian. "Seriously...*look* at yourself. Can't you *do* something about it?" he nagged.

"Do something? What do you want me to do?" asked Sarai.

"I don't know...squint a little. Maybe wear a veil or something."

"Don't be ridiculous. Every time the wind blows the thing will be flapping in my face. You worry too much."

"That's easy for you to say. What's the worst that can happen to you? You'll have some rich guy taking care of you. You'll be fine. But what about me? I'm a stranger here. What do you think happens to inconvenient husbands in a strange place? I'll tell you. They're murdered at the first available opportunity, that's what!"

When, just as he had anticipated, Sarai caught the eye of the Pharaoh himself, Abram was prepared. He pretended that she was his sister; it was the only prudent thing to do. In fact, he allowed the Pharaoh to take the reluctant Sarai into his house and into his bed, and was rewarded generously for his compliance. Having been convinced that only her silence would save her husband's life, Sarai resigned herself to obedience. Indeed, compared with Abram's self-serving acquiescence, the Pharaoh's lechery came to seem positively refreshing.

God apparently took exception to this convenient arrangement. Completely overlooking the fact that the whole scheme had been Abram's idea (being God, he must have known this), he contented himself with whipping up a nasty set of plagues to punish the unsuspecting Pharaoh for his part in the sorry affair.

"But I didn't know," protested the Pharaoh. "Why are you blaming me? They lied to me!"

God didn't care.

"You can't think I'm in the habit of marrying other men's wives...it's despicable!"

Understandably vexed at having been put in this compromising position, the Pharaoh had Abram and his family and possessions summarily ejected from Egypt. There's no indication that Abram ever considered returning the Pharaoh's gifts, but by then the disconcerted ruler was glad to get rid of him at any cost.

Sarai waited in vain to hear Abram thank her for allowing her body to be thus misused in his effort to protect his own skin. In fact, for some time he even pulled away from her touch, sulking over the thought that she had been handled by another man. When finally he found it in his heart to forgive her and opened his arms to her embrace, she was easily able to keep her enthusiasm within reasonable bounds.

Strangely, Abram retained his position as God's favourite.

They returned to the land of Canaan, but by now the family had grown so large that they agreed to split up, as the land could not sustain them all. Lot, who was Abram's nephew, chose to dwell in the plain of Jordan near the city of Sodom, while Abram and the rest of his family settled in Hebron. God, it appears, had given all the land thereabouts to Abram. It's impossible to be certain what arrangements The Lord had in mind for the people who already lived there when Abram arrived. Presumably they simply had to move aside.

In addition to wealth and protection, God had promised Abram that his descendants would inherit this land. Unfortunately Sarai appeared to be barren, so it seemed unlikely that there would *be* any descendants. However, Abram thought he might get away with fathering a child on her Egyptian handmaid, Hagar. He even tried to pretend that this was Sarai's idea, but she was no longer the naively obedient wife he had taken into Egypt. When she noticed that Hagar was pregnant and realized what had been going on under her own roof, Sarai stormed into his tent to avenge the indignity.

"How dare you?" she spat. "You've insulted me for the last time. You get her out of here. Do you think I'll stand by and let her brat inherit everything?"

"But," he stammered, "where can she go?"

"I don't give a damn...she can wander the desert, for all I care."

"But she'll die."

"Well, then, you'd better shift yourself to see that she doesn't. She goes today!"

Having already had his pleasure with Hagar, Abram was easily distracted by more pressing issues and barely lifted a finger to help the hapless Egyptian or the baby she would bear. (Well, that's not entirely true. He did provide her with a chunk of bread and a spare bottle of water. He even slung it over her shoulder with his own hands. That's just the kind of sensitive guy he was.)

What with wandering about and giving birth to the baby and all, poor Hagar used up all the water in no time. Being a tender-hearted soul, she couldn't bear to watch her infant son die of thirst, so she left him in the scant shade of a shrub, and wandered off a little way, in the hot sun, to await her own death. Fortunately, God was able to tear himself away from Abram's problems for a few moments to place a well in Hagar's path, saving her and the infant Ishmael in the nick of time. Being a slave and accustomed to harsh treatment, she was grateful for even this small favour and she doubtless spent the next several years explaining to Ishmael that his father was really a good man at heart and would have helped them out himself, if it hadn't been inconvenient for him to do so.

God still intended to give the land of Canaan to Abram and his descendants, to be theirs forever, but now he decided to attach a couple of conditions to the gift. "Abram, I want you to change your name," he said.

"My what?" blurted Abram. He hadn't been expecting a visit.

"Your name. I want you to change it."

"To what?"

"Abraham."

"Why?"

"Don't be impertinent. I don't have to explain myself to you. Just change it. To Abraham."

"OK." It seemed like a small price to pay for such an inheritance.

"And Sarai...I want her name to be Sarah from now on."

"I'll tell her."

As The Lord started to turn away, he had an amusing afterthought. "Oh...and there's something else."

"Sure. Anything at all."

"I want you and all your male descendants and slaves to have the flesh of your foreskins circumcised. In remembrance of our covenant. The inheritance, you know."

"You're kidding."

"No."

"We can't just promise to remember?"

"No. From now on, the foreskin of the uncircumcised will separate his soul from my Chosen People." And we are left to deduce from this where the souls of men are located.

This was one of the very few times God required anything painful or unpleasant of men which he did not require also of women. Perhaps he sensed that it would be hard to top the agony he had already inflicted on women by means of childbirth.

One day, when Abraham was relaxing in the doorway of his tent, God visited him. But as he was in a playful mood at the time, he did not appear as himself—he made himself look like three other guys. But Abraham recognized him (them?) immediately and, like a good host, he ran around getting everyone else to prepare refreshments. His supervisory skills must have pleased The Lord, who was inspired to promise that Abraham's wife would finally give birth to a son. When Sarah, who was every bit of ninety years old at the time, overheard this she laughed wryly to herself.

The Lord got a little miffed. "Do you doubt my power?" he asked, irritably.

"Oh, no. Not at all," replied Sarah, affably. "You are The Lord. You can do anything. A baby. I'm delighted!" She had simply been chuckling in eager anticipation of the fun labour and delivery that was in store for her in nine months' time. Abraham, unable to see what was so funny, peevishly ordered Sarah to exhibit her delight in some more seemly fashion before God changed his mind.

Soon God began hearing particularly nasty reports about the men of the cities of Sodom and Gomorrah. Based on the rumours alone, he had pretty much decided to destroy the cities unless fifty righteous people could be found within them. Abraham, recognizing this as a stacked deck, haggled until The Lord reduced the required number to a more realistic ten. Because this appeared to be a trouble zone, two of the more intrepid angels—they were all male at that time—were dispatched to conduct the search.

They were met at the gates of Sodom by Abram's nephew Lot, who hoped to present the city in its most favourable light. Fearing that their plan to sleep in the street might end badly, he insisted that the angels stay in his home instead. This did sound more comfortable but unfortunately they had already attracted the attention of the men of Sodom who encircled the house, demanding that they be sent out to feature in the nightly gang rape. Lot could see that this bit of local tomfoolery might reflect badly on his hospitality so he cast his eye about for a suitable alternative suggestion. His glance fell on his wife.

"Don't even think about it!" she warned.

Judging that the restive crowd outside was too numerous to be satisfied recycling a used matron, he didn't press the point. Thinking fast, he offered to send out his two virgin daughters instead, to be abused by the men in whatever ways suited their fancy.

A large, hairy brute in front spoke for the mob.

"Virgins," he said.

"Yes,' Lot assured him. "Quite untouched."

"Girls, then, you mean."

"Yes. My wife and I think they're very pretty...I know we're bound to be biased, being their parents, but..."

"I suppose it's too much to hope that you have a couple of pretty sons..."

"No. No sons. I'm sorry."

"Well...what do you expect us to do with *girls?"*

"Um...I thought..."

"No. You *didn't* think. You didn't think at all!"

The crowd behind him started to push forward.

"Some nerve!'

"He doesn't care what we want..."

"I bet he thinks he's *better* than us. We'll show him!"

"Yes...let's *show* him what we want." They surged forward. "Grab him!"

The angels, pulling him back into the house, barred the door barely in time to spare him a painful lesson in sexual diversity.

They apparently saw nothing objectionable in Lot's approach to the crisis. He had protected *their* asses, as it were, and isn't that the very least one could expect from a really considerate host? So they deftly blinded the evil men, enabling the ever so righteous Lot to escape with his family from wicked Sodom. They were convinced by then that they'd never find even ten righteous men in the city, so it was to be destroyed without further delay.

The angels ordered Lot and his family to flee to the neighbouring mountain without glancing back, while God rained fire and brimstone down on Sodom and Gomorrah, obliterating them completely. When Lot's wife peeked back to make sure the sorry place was actually gone, she was promptly turned into a pillar of salt...so we'd all remember, I suppose, that sacrificing virginity is alright, as long as you don't peek.

Left alone on that mountain with his two beautiful daughters and a singularly uncooperative salt pillar, Lot lost no time impregnating the girls...reasoning that God would surely want him to have sons to support him in his old age. He insisted afterwards that the saucy wenches had gotten him drunk and had their way with him, but then, blaming them was just the sort of altruistic gesture they had come to expect from their dear old dad.

Before long, Abraham again decided to head southward. But Sarah, despite her age, was still a fine looking woman and Abraham still imagined lechers lurking behind every bush, ready to slit his wrinkled old throat in order to carry her away. So, once again, he claimed that she was his sister and yet another king was taken in by the deception. This time it was Abimelech, king of the Philistines, who believed Abraham's story. Before he even had a chance to raise his nonagenarian bride's unusually heavy veil -we would be safe in assuming that she wore one by now, to hide any tell-tale wrinkles that ninety-odd years might have etched—God came knocking at his dreams, threatening to kill him for stealing another man's wife! Abimelech, like the Pharaoh before him, confronted Abraham, demanding an explanation.

"Well, she is my *half*-sister..." Abraham equivocated.

"But are you *married* to her?" persisted Abimelech.

"Actually ...um... yes. Didn't I mention that?" Abraham had no intention of admitting that he had used this ploy before—and would again, if the necessity arose.

Abimelech, fearing God's wrath and blaming himself for foolishly trusting Abraham, returned Sarah to her husband, and gave him servants, livestock, and a lot more money if he would only leave—with this sister and any other sisters that he might have concealed about his person—and never come back. Finally, he assuaged his crumpled ego by berating Sarah for allowing herself to be used in this tawdry fashion. Fortunately Sarah, at her advanced age, was way past being insulted by strangers. And she had come to expect it from Abraham.

As a reward for her part in this little deception, God allowed Sarah to conceive, and she bore a son they named Isaac. Being a good-humoured sort of woman, Sarah still thought it was pretty funny that she should be expected to not only give birth when in her nineties but also be grateful for the experience. She laughed a lot about that.

It was the custom of those days to sacrifice innocent animals, burning them on altars so that the scent of their cooked flesh might please The Lord. (The priests doubtless snacked on the leftovers after God had taken a good whiff, but he didn't seem to mind.) When his son Isaac was still a young boy, Abraham, who never tired of searching for ways to become even richer than he was already, developed a notion that God might be still more biased in his favour if he could only think of an unusually impressive item to sacrifice. He struggled to come up with a sufficiently thoughtful gift and in a moment of truly aberrant inspiration, he determined to sacrifice that which was most dear to him—his son. (Remember that he was over a hundred years old at the time and his mind may well have been slipping a cog from time to time.)

He set off with Isaac, a rope, a big stack of firewood—and a knife.

Fortunately he had confided his plan, in that garrulous way old men have, to Sarah. Thinking quickly, she surreptitiously followed him on a donkey, leading a fine ram which she'd been saving to serve at the next holiday feast. While he was tying Isaac atop the firewood on the altar, Sarah tethered the ram by its horns to a thorn bush and then hid herself nearby. As he raised the knife to cut Isaac's throat—she had waited, incredulously, to see whether he could really do this wicked thing—she disguised her voice as best she could, and called out, "Abraham, this is the angel of God speaking. You've proven your point. The Lord now knows how far you would go to show that you love and fear him, and is suitably impressed. It won't be necessary to actually slay and cook the boy. Look around, and I'm sure you can find something else to kill."

Even with his rheumy old eyes, Abraham couldn't fail to see the ram that Sarah had left practically under his nose, so he obediently sacrificed the poor animal and left it smouldering on the altar for God to smell to his heart's content...which may seem like a waste, but it still has to be seen as a big improvement on his original plan.

Sarah, her knees shaking from stress, rode back home on the ass she had brought, and found herself wondering whether she had not left a jackass behind. Perhaps this was due to the failing memory of old age, or maybe it was a flash of insight. In any case, she never quite recovered from this ordeal and died a few years later, having lingered long enough to see her son safely grown to manhood.

When yet another of those inconvenient famines drove Isaac, his wife Rebekah and their twin boys back into the lands of Abimelech, Isaac, like his father before him, developed the suspiciously convenient conviction that the Philistines were sure to covet his beautiful wife. Remembering the riches that Abraham had gained through a similar ruse, Isaac predictably broadcast the story that Rebekah was his sister, and waited eagerly to watch the marriage offers pour in. He hoped for at least a prince, but any particularly wealthy applicant would do. Rebekah, having heard the old stories, knew that this ploy was becoming widely derided as an embarrassing family habit, and she decided to put a stop to it. She showed no reluctance to being presented as Isaac's sister, but she took the first convenient opportunity to seduce him—right under the palace windows and in broad daylight.

"But someone will see," he protested.

"It'll be exciting," she purred, playfully. She loosened his robes and tousled his hair. "Don't be so prissy."

King Abimelech couldn't fail to notice them cavorting there on his own front lawn; it was easy to see they were a good deal closer than mere siblings had any right to be. The whole situation felt uncomfortably familiar. Determined not to be taken in again, he warned his people to keep their hands off both Rebekah and Isaac, who were obviously husband and wife. And just to be safe, he suggested that it might be a good idea to stay clear of their sheep and goats, as well. An end was put to the deception, Rebekah's honour was saved, Abimelech kept his money to himself...and Isaac had to find some other way to augment his already considerable fortune.

By the time Abraham had died and Isaac, too, was growing old, Rebekah began to be concerned about how the family wealth was to be managed after her husband's death. She herself was perfectly capable of handling the estate. She'd been doing it for years, as Isaac's energy failed. But she knew she would never formally be put in charge. Men had gotten the whole ownership thing all tied up for themselves long before then. Esau was Isaac's eldest son—older than his brother Jacob by perhaps a minute or two—and would, by tradition, inherit everything. While Rebekah loved both her sons, she had to admit to herself that Esau was not the sharpest tack in the box. Under his management, she feared, everything could be frittered away in no time.

Hoping she might have misjudged her 'eldest' son, she cooked up a mouth-watering soup. "Here." She gave it to Jacob. "I want you to let Esau catch a whiff of this. Tell him he can have it all, but only in exchange for his birthright."

"It'll never work, mom," Jacob protested. "Nobody would be foolish enough to give up a fortune in exchange for a bowl of soup...even if it's really *good* soup."

"One would think so," muttered Rebekah, grimly.

"Boy," He sniffed. "This is *really* good soup!"

When Esau returned, exhausted and famished, from the hunt—for he was a great hunter, being more than a mental match for dumb animals—the delicious odour brought him directly to Jacob's tent. "That smells great!" he bellowed, without preamble. "Dish me up a bowl."

"I don't think so," demurred Jacob.

"No kidding...I'm hungry. And it smells great. I want some."

"Not a chance. It's my favourite. I made it myself, and I'm going to eat it all. Get lost."

"Come on, please! Just one bowl. I've been out hunting all day, and I feel kind of faint...here...I'd better sit down. I don't know when I ate last...you know, it would look really bad if you let me starve to death right here in your tent." In fact, he had downed a substantial breakfast that morning, but he was feeling a bit dramatic.

"Well...all right. Look, I'll let you have it all. But only if you swear to give up your birthright."

"Sure...sure. Whatever. Where do you keep your bowls?"

"Wait." Jacob felt a small, sharp twinge. It may have been his conscience. "You know that means I'll inherit *everything...*"

At that moment, Esau was concerned with filling his belly. He didn't think his father would be dying any time soon, so it would be a long time before his birthright would become of any value to him. So he agreed without another thought, ate every drop of the soup, and felt that he'd made a pretty good bargain. Clearly, he had no knack for wealth management.

Rebekah now realized she must ensure that Jacob inherit the family properties if they were to have any chance at all of continued prosperity. Not only was tradition against her; Isaac also loved his elder son best. He fancied the venison feasts that Esau prepared after his hunting sprees, and these men obviously thought, in large part, with their stomachs. It would not be easy, but Rebekah was a *very* resourceful woman.

When Isaac, fearing he might be nearing the end of his life, decided to settle the inheritance, she overheard him telling Esau to hunt down some venison and cook up a celebratory stew, after which he would bless his eldest son and confirm his inheritance. Esau, completely forgetting his bargain with Jacob—in fact, he'd never given it a second thought—dashed off to do as his father bade.

Rebekah called Jacob to her tent. "Your father intends to give his inheritance to Esau." she warned. "Today."

"But I thought..." began Jacob

"There's no time for you to think. Just listen. You have to get to your father before Esau does. You'll have to convince him that *you* are Esau."

"But I don't even *look* like Esau."

"Oh, for heaven's sake...what difference does that make? He's quite blind by now. He'll never know the difference."

She felt no twinge of conscience about this, figuring it was a fair payback for the time Isaac had risked her honour by pretending to be her brother. Women held grudges for a long time, in those days. It was one of their few pleasures.

Being a superlative cook, she had no trouble spicing up some readily available goat meat to taste sufficiently like venison to deceive the jaded taste buds of her ancient husband.

But Jacob anticipated a potential flaw in her plan. "Dad may be blind, but he's not stupid. He knows that Esau is a lot hairier than I am. He's bound to notice." He really was much smarter than his brother.

Rebekah was undeterred. She covered his arms, hands and neck with the leftover goatskin, securely tied in place. He looked quite ridiculous, but since Isaac couldn't see anyway, it didn't much matter.

The plan went off without a hitch. Isaac, after feeling his son's hands to ensure that it was, indeed, the hairy Esau, blessed him and promised him the inheritance.

When Esau arrived, having found, killed and cooked some prime venison, he found that Isaac had already given away both his blessing and the inheritance to an impostor. Belatedly remembering the bargain he'd made with his brother, Esau had no doubt that the trickster was Jacob. He begged his father to scrape together another blessing for him—even a little one would do—and a small share of the property would be nice too. But Isaac, while he regretted the mistake, had eaten his fill and now considered the matter to be closed, so Esau was out of luck. Jacob would be the head of the family with authority over all his siblings...and that included his older brother. Esau was not so stupid that he didn't know he'd been robbed, and he vowed to kill Jacob as soon as his father was dead and a suitable period of mourning had been observed.

As soon as Rebekah heard of this threat, she began scheming to get Jacob out of harm's way until Esau's anger cooled. While she pondered, she started cooking. It couldn't hurt.

She entered Isaac's tent bearing yet another tasty treat. "I thought you might like a snack." She drooped down beside him, and sighed.

Between mouthfuls, he noticed her dejection. "What's the problem?" he asked, finally.

"Oh, it's nothing." She sighed again. "I don't want to bother you."

"This dish is superb. One of your best," he stated. "It's no bother...what's the matter?"

"Well, Jacob will be searching for a wife soon, and he's sure to choose a local girl."

"Yes. So?"

"I don't like them."

"Which ones don't you like? Surely he can choose from among the others."

"I dislike them all."

"All of them? You don't like any of them? Why, for heaven's sake?"

"I don't know. I just can't tolerate them. They have all these annoying...*habits*. He'll marry one, and she'll be under foot all the time with her irritating, unfamiliar habits and I simply won't be able to function. I'm sure it will spoil my cooking..."

Isaac had begun to lose interest, but this caught his attention. "I won't have you upset, my dear. Give me a moment. I'm sure I'll think of something."

Eventually, he hit on the obvious solution. Jacob must make a trip to Mesopotamia to choose a wife from among Rebekah's relatives: girls more likely to have unobjectionable, *familiar* habits. His crafty wife pretended to be both surprised at this clever solution and touched by his consideration on her behalf, and quickly rushed Jacob out of town on his wife-hunting trek.

Hearing that his mother disliked all the neighbourhood girls, Esau also dutifully searched out a wife from among their many relatives; but by that time nobody much cared, especially since he was already married to a couple of the local cuties. Poor Esau—forever fated to come in a day late and a dollar short.

If Jacob thought this trip was going to shape up to be just another pleasure jaunt, he was very much mistaken. Having sought out his mother's family, he promptly fancied himself head-over-heels in love with his beautiful cousin Rachel. Unfortunately, his uncle Laban had a pretty shrewd idea of his daughter's market value, and no sentimental childhood memories of his sister Rebekah prevented him from driving a hard bargain with her son. Jacob was so besotted that he agreed to work for Laban for seven long years in order to earn Rachel's hand in marriage. Furthermore, when this time had elapsed, and the eager Jacob prepared to claim his long-awaited prize, the crafty Laban managed to slip Rachel's not-so-beautiful older sister Leah into Jacob's bed instead. The romantic Jacob, who had been celebrating rather heartily, was so drunk he didn't notice until it was too late. None too pleased with this bait-and-switch, he now found himself obliged to work for Laban yet another seven years in order to marry Rachel as well.

The ever-so-desirable Rachel had been quite young when Jacob first arrived, bringing with him the glamour that distance imparts to strangers. She was dazzled by the evidence of his affection and flattered to find that he was prepared to labour for seven long years in order to win her. It made her feel special. Now, seven years later, her drunken bridegroom had spent the wedding night with someone else, and not even known the difference. She was not nearly so young any more, and she felt a whole lot less special.

And what about Leah? She had been foisted on Jacob like an inferior slab of meat, slipped into a package in the marketplace by a dishonest trader. She, too, did not feel so very special.

Neither sister retained any romantic illusions about this marriage. But they were stuck in it, together. This did not bring them closer.

Apparently Laban was willing to agree to something resembling a lay-away plan, because during this second seven years, Jacob was permitted to sleep with both Leah and Rachel—as well as their handmaidens, for a touch of additional variety. It seems the time passed pleasantly enough for Jacob, who fathered several progeny on these various women, and any friction this may have caused between the wives was not allowed to inconvenience him in any significant way. Finally, after twenty years, Jacob took his extensive family as well as a major share of the livestock in lieu of back wages, and left for his homeland.

Nearing his old home, Jacob heard that Esau was coming to meet him accompanied by four hundred of his closest friends, and he worried that this might not be the welcome wagon. Just to be safe, he sent servants on ahead with droves of livestock as a peace offering. When Esau saw that Jacob had returned with servants and cattle of his own and, far from being a drain on the resources of the patrimony, had brought back souvenirs for all, he generously welcomed his brother with open arms. They agreed that there was wealth enough for both, and Jacob settled down with his household somewhere in the neighbourhood...avoiding the plot right next door. (That might have put unnecessary stress on their relationship, which had already taken about all the strain it could stand).

With the passing of time, Jacob's family adjusted enthusiastically to their new home. His daughter Dinah visited with the local girls which also brought her to the attention of their brothers. Amid this gay social whirl, she met Shechem, son of a local Canaanite prince, who swept her off her feet and into his bed—or somewhere equally cozy. Finding that she was as congenial in private as she was in public, he fell in love and sent his father to Jacob to request her hand in marriage. Unfortunately, in presenting to Jacob the reasons why such a match was desirable, the prince indiscreetly revealed the fact that the young couple had already tested and proven their sexual compatibility. Jacob and all Dinah's brothers were horrified that Shechem had already sampled the goods—and long before they had received any bridal fee whatever! They felt used and defiled.

And yet, they seemed strangely acquiescent when it was suggested that the young people of Canaan be allowed to marry freely with Jacob's sons and daughters in the future. "I think we can agree to that," said Jacob, "as long as our traditions are respected."

The Canaanites were delighted. Jacob was a very wealthy man.

"Of course," Jacob demurred, "our daughters could not be expected to marry any men who have not gotten circumcised..."

"Oh, naturally we would be willing...uh...what's circumcised, and how do we get it?"

"Our men have their foreskins removed. It's done when they're still babies...a simple operation."

The Canaanite men all blanched. Every one. "Can't an exception be made," they pleaded, "in the interest of diversity?"

"Sorry. We can't negotiate on this one. It's a deal breaker."

Seeing Jacob's fortune slipping from their grasp, the Canaanites reluctantly agreed.

Now, no one had pointed out to them the fact that this particular operation, which was relatively minor in infancy, could be uncomfortable when performed on grown men. No matter—they found out soon enough. But they had little time to regret their decision because while they hobbled around, weak and whiney, two of Dinah's brothers murdered every last one of them including Shechem, not neglecting to loot and pillage and take the residual Canaanite women for themselves.

On their return, Jacob sensed that they might have gone a little too far in their righteous anger over the seduction of their sister. (The looting may have put it over the top...after all, they had already collected a lot of nifty bridal gifts). He feared that the other inhabitants of the neighbourhood might think badly of him and, in those days, that could result in some serious retaliatory destruction. He consulted The Lord, who wisely advised him to pack up and move on—fast.

Through all this, no one had even once bothered to ask Dinah what *she* wanted. It was a matter of honour:

her brothers' honour...and maybe her father's. Actually Dinah had rather liked Shechem, or she wouldn't have accepted his advances in the first place. He had loved her and treated her a good deal better than her own family ever had. In fact, she considered her brothers to be a couple of bloodthirsty, avaricious asses—but, as I said, nobody asked her.

It was at about this time that God dropped in on Jacob with a complaint. "I thought we agreed that you would start calling yourself Israel."

"I keep forgetting."

"How would you like it if I forgot to save that land I promised you?"

"I'm sorry. I'll try harder."

"You do that. I want the nation you're founding to be called Israel. Jacobland simply doesn't have the right ring to it."

Jacob was getting pretty old by this time, and never did get comfortable with the new name, although he took care to use it on all important legal documents.

Jacob loved Rachel's son Joseph, who was his youngest at that time, more than all his other offspring. Not being noticeably more sensitive than was typical of the men in his family, he took no pains to hide his preference.

Rachel saw that he was spoiling the boy and drew his attention to the resentment that was growing against Joseph among his overlooked siblings but Jacob wouldn't listen. Flaunting his right, as their father, to do as he pleased, he insisted that Rachel weave for Joseph a new and stylish coat: a blatant symbol of his favouritism.

"And make it nicer than all the other boys' coats."

"Fine," shrugged Rachel. "What colour do you want it to be?"

"Pink."

"Pink?"

"Pink."

"Are you sure?"

"Sure...what's wrong with pink?"

"Well...pink might not be...helpful. A pink coat. I don't think so."

"So put in a bit of purple."

"Pink and purple."

"Yeah. And green...I like green."

"Hmmm...okay..."

"Can you add yellow?"

"I have yellow thread..."

"Yellow will be nice. Look...what colours do you have? Put them all in. Make stripes."

"Of course. Stripes. Why not?" Rachel sighed and got to work, muttering something caustic about men and fashion sense.

Joseph, who kept himself constantly in the limelight by tattling on his brothers at every opportunity (not a habit likely to win great popularity), revelled in this new chance to demonstrate his father's regard. His presence, in his flashy new duds, became extremely odious to them.

Furthermore, it was not enough for Joseph to be his father's darling. He wanted his brothers to give him respect he had done absolutely nothing to earn.

"I had a wonderful dream," he told them.

"Who cares?" they growled, sullenly.

"No, really," he insisted. "You have to hear this...the sun, the moon and eleven stars were all bowing down to me!" The meaning of this dream was about as subtle as a sledge hammer, and it only served to make his brothers resent him all the more. Moreover, he made the mistake of repeating the dream to his father. Jacob's doting fondness was temporarily eclipsed by his irritation at the obvious image of himself, his wife and his strapping sons bowing down to this presumptuous seventeen-year-old stripling. A smart smack alongside the head rendered Joseph a trifle more humble, but it didn't allay his brothers' jealousy one bit.

The next time Joseph was sent out into the countryside to check on the whereabouts of his brothers and the flocks they were tending, they stripped him of the offending coat and threw him down into a pit, then sold him to the first caravan of Ishmaelite traders that happened by. This had not been the most popular choice of action but murder, which had been strongly advocated by the majority, would not have put welcome shekels in their pockets, so the more practical voices among them prevailed. They were ready to blame it all on a roving band of evil Midianite businessmen but their purses jingled suspiciously with their ill-gotten gains...and they all knew the truth. Craftily covering their crime, they ripped the coat, smeared it artistically with goat blood, and carried it home.

Jacob recognized the garment immediately. "It has to be Joseph's coat," he cried. "It has at least five more colours than any other coat in the neighbourhood." He assumed that his beloved son had been torn apart by wild animals, and he was inconsolable.

In his extreme grief, he insisted that the day of Joseph's disappearance be commemorated by the family. "Each year," he sobbed, "I want you to rip up your finest garment as a token of your sorrow."

Rachel failed to see how this would benefit her unfortunate son. "Don't you think it might be wiser to just put on our shabbiest clothes for a while, and rub dirt on them?" It wasn't quite as dramatic, but it was less wasteful and Jacob found he could be as sad in dirty sackcloth as he would have been in expensive rags.

Rachel, too, mourned her son—deeply, if not so ostentatiously. She was so upset that she almost failed to notice the unusual wealth with which Jacob's remaining sons appeared to be consoling themselves for the loss of their brother. And the shifty way they avoided her eye.

Women were valued highly in those days—not as highly as the least of men, of course, but well above the worth of all but the most superior livestock. Their value rested primarily in their ability to bring forth offspring: *male* offspring. And once a family had purchased a maiden with potential, it was most definitely not about to let her get away. After Jacob's son Judah had procured a sturdy, unblemished wife named Tamar for his eldest son, the lad committed some crime so heinous that God slew him *with his own hands*, and wouldn't even say why. The girl was left widowed, childless and bewildered.

Rather than risk losing the child-bearing potential of this prime piece of breeding stock, Judah passed her along to his second son, Onan, incidentally saving himself an additional bride-price. Well, Onan had spent his whole life making do with his older brother's leftovers, and he'd had enough of it. If he couldn't have a brand new, off-the-shelf bride of his own, he would simply do without. So he turned his back on Tamar and their marital bed, and relieved his itch with his own right hand, spilling his seed on the ground rather than in the receptacle nature had provided for the purpose. Poor Tamar was humiliated, which didn't matter in the least. But God was apparently sufficiently offended by this waste of resources to slay this second husband in his turn.

Stubbornly determined not to forfeit his investment, Judah now resolved to wed the unfortunate widow to his third son who was, regrettably, just a child at the time. Undaunted, he sent her away to await the boy's maturity in the home of her parents. Years passed and the lad grew to manhood, but by then Judah had forgotten all about Tamar, much as one might forget about a valuable piece of clothing if it's tucked away in the back of a closet for too long.

Recognizing that her only acknowledged value was as a brood-mare, Tamar devised a plan. The next time Judah was in the neighbourhood, she tricked herself out as a prostitute and, disguised in a veil, posed seductively in the marketplace. She didn't have to wait long. Like many another man away from home on a business trip, Judah was ill prepared to resist temptation.

When his eye fell on this tempting morsel, he didn't suspect for a moment that it could be Tamar. "What's your price?" he asked.

"Make me an offer," purred the intriguingly veiled figure.

"How about a healthy young goat...?"

She eyed him up and down. "I see no *young* goat here."

Undeterred, he admitted that he didn't have any spare goats with him at the time, but he offered his jewellery as collateral.

"But the veil stays," she insisted, coyly.

"Whatever." His eyes had, long since, left her face, and he had no immediate plans to return them to that vicinity. A bargain was struck for a night of her time, and they got down to business.

When he subsequently sent his servant with a goat, to retrieve the pledge, the prostitute and his jewellery were nowhere to be found. Feeling like a rube, he cursed the pitfalls designed by the contemporary world to ensnare a godly man like himself and promptly put the whole episode out of his mind.

Soon he began to hear rumours that his daughter-in-law had prostituted herself, and was pregnant. Naturally, he was outraged.

When the young woman (well, not so very young by this time) was brought before him for sentencing, Judah put on his most sanctimonious face. "What you have been accused of is the vilest of sins: a sin against my family and a sin against God. You deserve to die...you and the reprobates who have consorted with you. But you alone are my responsibility. I condemn you to be burnt to death...just as soon as it can be conveniently arranged."

He had the most uncomfortable feeling that something was not as it should be. Tamar, who should, by rights, have been cowering abjectly at his feet, was strangely composed. In fact, she gave the appearance of being comfortably relaxed—perhaps even a touch scornful—and a tiny enigmatic smile hovered at the corners of her lips. It was disconcerting.

"How can you...have you no remorse, you vile creature?" he stammered, in his confusion.

Tamar stepped forward and held out her hand, seemingly in supplication. Looking straight into his eyes and without a word, she turned her hand over and dropped several pieces of jewellery in the dirt at his feet. It was *very* distinctive jewellery. It was *his* jewellery.

Somehow, the transgression looked a lot less serious when he realized that he had been an active participant, so Judah quietly dropped the whole bonfire idea. When Tamar gave birth to twin boys, she was swiftly accepted back as a respected member of the family so that Judah could reap the return on his investment. And though she never did get the kid he had promised, at least the old goat steered clear of her in the future, so she was content.

When the Ishmaelites who had purchased Joseph passed through Egypt, they sold him to Potiphar, an officer of the Pharaoh. The boy displayed a talent for management, and it didn't take Potiphar long to notice that everything Joseph put his hand to prospered. Eventually he was put in charge of the whole household, and he ran it with remarkable efficiency.

His life would have been a comfortable one, had it not been for Potiphar's wife. She was a nasty piece of work, shrill and vain. She draped her robes much too low in the front, wore entirely too much make-up, and had a dangerous fondness for attractive young men. Before long Joseph caught her eye, but when she tried to seduce him he hastily declined on the grounds that it would be a betrayal of trust. Refusing to take no for an answer, she cast subtlety aside and tried to drag him to her bed by main force.

"What are you doing?" he squeaked. His young voice still tended to slide up an octave or so when he was distressed. "Get off me! You're not bad looking for your age... but I'm just not *into* older women." (Remember that he was never notable for tact and sensitivity.) "You might have better luck with the gardener...or maybe one of the older stable boys," he suggested.

He wrenched himself away and, leaving his robe in her grasp, he bolted in nothing but his second-best underwear. He had not been anticipating this unusual level of exposure when he dressed himself that morning.

Enraged and humiliated, the scorned woman screamed rape, and showed his discarded robe in her bedroom as proof of the crime. This was enough to convince Potiphar, who preferred that explanation to any other that came to mind. He immediately had Joseph imprisoned. Joseph learned two important things from this setback. He learned to tie his robe a lot tighter—and he learned that sometimes it's wise to treat people a little more diplomatically...especially when they're women of a certain age. They're wily, and they can be vindictive.

Always looking for an angle, while he was in prison Joseph set up shop as an interpreter of dreams. He built up quite a reputation, the competition being somewhat limited, so when the Pharaoh himself was troubled by a couple of strange dreams, it was suggested that he consult the young Hebrew—by then, Joseph's people were known as Hebrews—for an explanation.

Joseph appeared before Pharaoh and listened carefully to the dreams. The first was about seven fat and healthy cattle feeding in a meadow. Seven lean and scrawny cattle came out of the river and, in a manner rather uncharacteristic of livestock, ate the fat ones—every last one. The second dream was much like the first, but with corn.

Joseph put on his most convincingly sincere thinking face for the Pharaoh's benefit, and allowed a few tense minutes to pass as he considered his reply. "The both dreams are so similar," he said, "that I can give you two for the price of one. They clearly predict seven years of plenty, throughout Egypt..."

Some of the more junior courtiers began to cheer and whistle in an inappropriately undignified manner.

"...followed by seven years of famine."

The faces of all the courtiers fell, as if they actually cared. Pharaoh graciously thanked Joseph for the warning.

"Always glad to be of service," replied Joseph, "but I simply translate the message. God sent the dreams—and He's not kidding!" He added that the smart move would be to appoint a really good manager over the whole country to handle this approaching crisis in such a way as to avoid causing the busy Pharaoh any unnecessary inconvenience. When Pharaoh cast his eyes about, searching for just such a clever manager, it's no surprise that Joseph caught his eye—standing, as he was, right in front of him at the time. Congratulating himself on this remarkable serendipity, Pharaoh appointed Joseph to supervise all Egypt henceforth. This was a pretty good gig for Joseph, who was ambitious and had been waiting for a good opportunity to expand operations beyond the prison walls.

For the next seven years of bumper harvests, Joseph caused all excess food to be set aside in royal storehouses. Then, when famine struck the land in the eighth year, exactly as predicted, he opened the storehouses and made the food available to the hungry people. To be more exact, he sold the food to the hungry people, and at substantially inflated prices. Joseph made a fortune on these transactions, but Pharaoh was so glad he didn't have a disaster to deal with that he pretended not to notice.

The famine that had been aimed at Egypt also affected the surrounding lands, including Canaan. Lacking prophetic dreams and a good economist, Jacob had been unable to anticipate the shortage and the family feasts began to look somewhat meagre. The rumour that there was food available in Egypt eventually reached him, and Jacob optimistically sent most of his remaining sons off to buy provisions. His youngest, Benjamin, had been born to Rachel since Joseph's disappearance, but he was now the favourite and was kept at home.

When the brothers approached Joseph to purchase corn, he recognized them immediately. They, on the other hand, had no idea at all who *he* was. They bowed down before him (does this sound familiar?) and obligingly answered his eager questions about their father and their home. Learning of their youngest brother, he developed a passionate desire to see him, and sent them home to fetch Benjamin to Egypt. Since he made it clear that only this would ensure a refill of corn, it was simply a matter of time and hunger until they returned with the youngster.

As soon as Joseph saw the lad, he was affected to the point of tears, but he decided to have a little fun at their expense anyway. It may be that he was still a wee bit irritated at them for selling him into slavery. So when they had made their necessary purchases and were preparing to leave, he instructed his steward to conceal his favourite silver cup in young Benjamin's pack.

"Now," he ordered, after they were well on their way, "I want you to send a troop of soldiers after the Israelites. It doesn't have to be my best men. They won't put up any resistance."

"I'll inform the commander of your orders right away."

"Tell the soldiers to search their baggage. I think my favourite cup is missing."

"But...I just put the cup..."

"Yes, yes, I know. It won't be hard to find. It'll be in the pack of the youngest."

"Well...what should they do when they find it?" asked the confused steward.

"Accuse the lad of robbery, of course. Then bind him as a slave, and drag him back to be punished." Joseph chuckled playfully.

After he'd entertained himself by watching his brothers beg and grovel and plead for Benjamin's freedom for a while, Joseph revealed who he really was, and they all had a good laugh about it. Except maybe Benjamin, who was still shaken by the experience. Being rather young, it would take him some time to adjust to Joseph's winning ways. Joseph spent some time bragging about how he'd saved them all from starvation then sent them to bring Jacob and his whole household to live in Egypt and share his good fortune.

He didn't remember to ask about his mother and they didn't think to mention her. In fact, she had died soon after giving birth to Benjamin and they had all, long since, forgotten her. There had been so many mothers...

The offspring of Joseph and his eleven brothers were destined to form the twelve tribes of Israel.

Chapter 3

The Exodus

Long after Joseph and his influence had been forgotten by the Pharaohs, the Hebrews remained in Egypt, multiplying as fruitfully as ever. With Joseph's help they prospered, and naturally enough, the succeeding Pharaohs became concerned at the potential power of these foreign people living amongst them, so they conscripted the Hebrews to work at major municipal construction in the Public Works department.

They were driven hard, and they became poor enough to suit anyone, but their numbers still increased at an alarming rate.

Finally, a reigning Pharaoh felt he had a simple solution. Feeling pretty smug, he summoned the leading Hebrew midwives.

"I'm instituting a new policy," he said, "and I've chosen you to implement it."

The Chamberlain piped in: "Special assignment from the Pharaoh, ladies...great honour..."

The women waited, silently. Life had made them suspicious of such honours.

"Here's what I want you to do," instructed the Pharaoh. "I want you to kill all Hebrew babies at birth—or before, if you can manage it. But be discreet. I don't want the mothers to know. They'd be sure to make a fuss. Any questions?"

There was a horrified silence. Then one of the older, bolder women stepped forward. "We can't do that!" she blurted.

"Okay, okay," conceded the Pharaoh. "Just the boys, then. You're dismissed. Help yourselves to refreshments in the anteroom on your way out." He turned away to discuss the plan revision with the Chamberlain and the women found themselves hustled out by a minion who had been hovering there for exactly that purpose.

The midwives, however, could not bring themselves to kill the innocent baby boys. For a while, the Hebrews pretended that all newborns were merely stunted toddlers who had been born before Pharaoh's decree. But eventually, the continued appearance of suspiciously small male Hebrews was noticed and the midwives were summoned to give an explanation.

"It has come to my attention," observed the Pharaoh, "that a lot of baby boys appear to be slipping past you ladies. I'd like to hear an explanation."

"Of course," offered the same old midwife who had dared to address Pharaoh the last time. "Here's one: our Hebrew women are so much more vigorous than your delicate Egyptians that the babies simply popped out before we were able to interfere. How's that?"

Pharaoh was not amused.

He quickly threw together a new plan, and demanded that all the newborn Hebrew boys be immediately thrown into the river to drown.

He hadn't reckoned on the decency of his own Egyptian women who were appalled. Refusing to countenance this brutal decree, they conspired secretly with the Hebrew women to save the innocent babies. The Hebrew mothers, indeed, committed their newborn sons to the river but they floated them in cleverly constructed waterproof baskets while the soft-hearted Egyptian women watched vigilantly down-stream, fishing the babies out of the water as they floated by and raising them as their own...defying their own husbands to betray the secret.

When the Pharaoh's daughter noticed that all the other women had one, she just had to have a Hebrew baby of her own.

"Fish me out a cute one," she told her attendants. "A boy would be nice..."

When they found one that met with her approval, she named him Moses and raised him in luxury, lavishing every affection on him as though he were her own son.

By the time Moses was full grown, this over-indulgent environment had combined with his headstrong nature to create a volatile personality. While meddling in an altercation in defence of a Hebrew worker, he carelessly killed an Egyptian overseer and fled into the desert to escape punishment. His foster mother was inconsolable at his disappearance, but now that he had alienated himself from the Egyptians, Moses conveniently realized that he was himself a Hebrew by birth and didn't give her another moment's thought.

Settling in the land of Midian, he married Zipporah, the daughter of Jethro the priest, and became shepherd to his father-in-law's herds. One day, when Moses was tending the flock at the mountain of Horeb, he saw a bush that appeared to be burning...but it was not consumed by the fire. Intrigued, he approached to have a closer look. A voice which introduced itself as God warned him to keep his distance. (Sometimes, when you make a bush burn in that unique fashion, you don't want people to examine it too closely.)

"You must have noticed how hard the Hebrews are made to work by their Egyptian masters," said God. "They don't like it. I'm sending you to bring them away from there and into a land of milk and honey. There are a lot of other people living there now, actually, but I'm going to give it to the Hebrews anyway. I promised them I would, quite some time ago. I didn't exactly forget..." he added, somewhat apologetically, "I've just been busy with other things."

"I'm flattered," answered Moses. "I really am. But are you sure I'm the right man for this? I'm not so sure the Hebrews would be so very eager to follow me. I mean...I could be recognized. Some of them might still remember me from my life as an Egyptian oppressor...and then there's still that murder thing..."

"Oh, don't worry about that," God assured him. "That old murder rap is a cold case. Everybody who cared about it is dead by now. And I can teach you a few signs that will be sure to convince both the Hebrews and the Egyptians to take you seriously."

Still Moses hesitated, expressing serious doubts about his untried public speaking skills, but The Lord, detecting an unseemly lack of enthusiasm for the project, began to get impatient.

"Isn't Aaron, the Levite, your brother? Well, *he* can talk a blue streak. If you're going to lead this thing—and you *are*—then you've got to start making executive decisions. Recruit Aaron. He can handle the public speaking portion of the program while you manage the Revealing Signs.

"Now, get moving, and we'll meet again here at the mountain when you're done."

Loading Zipporah and his sons on an ass, Moses set off for Egypt, picking up Aaron on the way. Unfortunately, in making the transition from acting Egyptian to devout Hebrew, he had neglected to attend to the circumcision of his first-born son. God was quick to notice the omission. As a playful reminder, The Lord ambushed Moses at a wayside inn, and attempted to kill him. (No details are available regarding the form the assassination attempt took, nor—what's more fascinating—how it could possibly have failed.) Moses was at a loss to understand where he might have transgressed...his mission was barely *started.*

Knowing how fond God was of these little tokens of submission, Zipporah grabbed the nearest sharp stone, deftly hacked off her son's foreskin (we can only hope that the lad was still quite young at the time) and threw it at Moses' feet.

"There!" she spat. *"You* give it to Him. And you'd better make it a Celebration, or we'll never hear the end of it." She comforted the screaming child. "You'd think it could have waited until we were settled." she muttered, "How much gear does He think I can *pack* on one ass...?"

When Moses reached Egypt, he approached Pharaoh with his demands. "You may not be aware that there's a Hebrew feast coming up," he began. "My people are going to need a three-day holiday."

The Pharaoh stared at him. "No," he replied.

"But it's in honour of our God," Moses protested.

"And yet...I don't care."

"I'm afraid I'm going to have to insist."

"Who *are* you? Get out of my palace!" snapped the Pharaoh. "No, wait! You can take a message to your

Hebrews. Up to now, in the interest of efficiency, I've provided them with straw for the manufacture of bricks. No more. From now on, they can scrounge for the straw themselves. See how they like *that.* And they'd better produce not a brick less, if they know what's good for them." Pharaoh turned to his chief of guards. "Now, get him out of here."

Moses returned to his people and tried to put a positive spin on the meeting.

"Our preliminary negotiations have been concluded, and we've achieved some major changes to your contract!" He tried to look as victorious as possible under the circumstances.

When they heard the details, the Hebrews were somewhat disillusioned with Moses. "Brilliant!" they spat, sarcastically. "You've just gone and made everything worse."

Aaron, being the fast talker of the family, convinced them that it was all part of a comprehensive plan, and he and Moses went back to Pharaoh to give it another try.

This time they tried a couple of their signs, but they had decided it would be more dignified for Aaron to do the physical stuff while Moses managed the show. Accordingly, Aaron started with a flourish by turning his brother's staff into a snake and transforming river water into blood at Moses' direction.

Pharaoh's magicians scoffed. "That old 'staff into a snake' stunt...big deal! And we stopped using that river transformation bit years ago. It kills off all the fish and makes the river smell bad. But if you insist...watch this!"

Unfortunately for Moses, the magicians did appear to be able to duplicate these marvels, so it all simply looked like a second-rate parlour trick and Pharaoh was unimpressed. And to make things worse, some of the snakes appeared to slither off into the most inconvenient palace nooks and crannies, frightening the servants and a few of the younger courtesans. Naturally, Pharaoh blamed Moses for the disruption, and once more had him ejected from the palace.

Now God really began to put the pressure on. He sent swarms of frogs and lice and flies and locusts to bite and destroy and die and stink. He made boils appear on the Egyptians (but not the Hebrews) and killed the livestock of the Egyptians (but not the Hebrews). And he sent hail and darkness to torment and frighten the Egyptians (but not the Hebrews in their midst; this selective application of hail and darkness was tricky, but not beyond the power of God, of course). With each affliction, Pharaoh promised to release the Hebrews from their bondage if only Moses would make it stop. But each time Moses complied, Pharaoh broke his promise and refused to let the Hebrews go.

Finally, God sent a plague to kill all the firstborn of Egypt and Pharaoh, whose favourite son had been stricken along with all the rest, ordered the Hebrews to pack their belongings and get out of Egypt.

The Hebrew women had suspected that once they were allowed to leave, they would be expected to vacate without a moment's delay, so while the men had a quick celebratory feast, their wives feverishly baked bread, unleavened as it was, to eat *en route*, and they all slept in their traveling clothes. They barely had time to borrow as much jewellery and clothing as their Egyptian neighbours could be prevailed upon to lend them before they stole away into the wilderness in the dark of night.

When the Egyptians realized that the Hebrews had hurriedly departed without returning the borrowed property they, sadly, interpreted this as theft and took serious offence. In fact, Pharaoh went so far as to dispatch his army to apprehend them.

"It won't be hard to find them," he assured his generals. "Just keep your eyes open for a group of about six hundred thousand people, following a guy with a staff. There'll be a lot of children and a fair number of old folks, so they won't be moving very fast."

He was quite right. The Hebrews were traveling on foot and were slowed down significantly by all their livestock as well as the burden of their household goods, without even considering the additional weight of their borrowed finery.

They traveled both by day, led by a pillar of cloud, and by night, lit by a pillar of flame. But by the time they reached the shores of the Red Sea, Pharaoh's army was hot on their heels. Many of the Hebrews who had been lukewarm about this venture expressed their dismay at finding themselves trapped between an unfriendly army and the unwelcoming waves.

"Surely," they complained, "there were grave sites enough back there to accommodate all applicants. There was no need for us to scurry across the countryside in order to find a place to die!"

Ignoring the perceptible touch of sarcasm in their observation, Moses confidently stretched out his arm, and God sent a strong east wind to hold back the sea so that the Hebrews could walk across upon the muddy sea bed—grubby work, to be sure, but a huge improvement over the available alternatives.

While the men gazed in awe at this miracle and congratulated Moses on his impressive arm-stretching, the women discussed the logistical challenge facing them.

"Just look at that muck."

"It's a long way across."

"With all our household goods loaded on these few carts, the wheels will sink to their axles in no time. We'll never make it across. We're going to have to jettison a lot of this stuff, and carry the rest."

"Damn! Well, we may as well get started. Call the men over here."

"Are you kidding? It'll be a fiasco. Who knows what junk they'll insist on keeping? One thing for sure: anything in the least useful will get thrown aside! Besides, we supervised the packing...we know where to find the most essential things. We'll have to sort it out ourselves."

Before they were much more than half way through the unpacking, a few of the men noticed the flurry of activity at the carts. "What do you think you're doing?" they demanded. "We have to get going. You can't search for your little fripperies at a time like this!"

"Don't be ridiculous." The women continued working feverishly. "We're doing some serious downsizing. The wagons will never make it through that mire. We can only take the bare necessities."

"We have to leave the wagons? How will we get our stuff across?"

"We'll just have to carry it."

"You're kidding!"

"Do I look like I'm kidding? Tell Moses to get over here and roll up his sleeves on the way."

"Wait! Since when do you women tell us what to do? The elders need time to debate all facets of this issue then we'll get back to you with a decision."

There *was* no time. The wall of sea water could crash back at any moment. The women, grabbing up heavy pots and sacks of food, hurried off for the other shore.

"They're going anyway," observed one of the more perceptive men.

"Without us," noted another.

"That stuff looks awfully heavy. Some of them are practically bent double. Look at that old one over there."

Silence fell.

Then: "This is kind of embarrassing. Maybe we should help."

"Well, now that I notice, that water is beginning to look pretty precarious...and those Egyptians behind us seem a lot more hostile than I remember them."

Leaving the carts and the knick-knacks behind, they shouldered the remaining necessities and scrambled off after their women.

The army attempted to pursue them, but when the last Hebrew had reached the opposite shore Moses signalled for the waters to return. The Egyptian chariot wheels had become mired in the mud, making escape impossible, so the Hebrews were able to watch, chuckling, as every last soldier was drowned. After Moses had composed a celebratory song and his sister Miriam had led the women in a gay little impromptu dance, they proceeded on their way with fresh respect for their leader and a renewed fear of God's deadly power.

Moses had agreed to meet The Lord back at the Mount of Horeb in Midian after rescuing the Hebrews from bondage. However, he'd chosen the long route home, so when they arrived at Mount Sinai after traveling three months in the wilderness, he figured that one mount was much like another and climbed up. Sure enough, God was up there, and wanted to talk to him—but privately. So he sent word that no one except Moses was to set foot on the mount, on pain of death. He provided a good show for the rest in the way of thunder and lightning, smoke and fire and trumpets, and even spoke a few words in his own voice, but only Moses was allowed to actually see him...and then it was only a quick glimpse of his hind parts as he walked away. (Clearly, God did not habitually wear robes in those formative days but full frontal nudity was a familiarity at which he absolutely drew the line.)

"I hope you people realize that you would never have escaped Egypt without my help." The Lord flung these words over his shoulder as he left. "You owe me."

This was true enough; Moses spent a few moments thinking appropriately grateful thoughts then began to wonder whether the interview might be over. But when he was once again decently hidden, God revealed two stone tablets upon which he had written, with his own finger, ten of his favourite commandments. Admitting candidly that he had an unfortunate tendency toward jealousy, he forbade the people to worship other gods—in fact, he mentioned this twice, specifically forbidding the worship of graven images—and he warned them not to swear by his name unless they really meant it. He insisted that they keep every seventh day as a day of rest (he didn't expect to see much resistance to this), and instructed them to honour their fathers and mothers, whether they deserved it or not. Killing and adultery and stealing and perjury...all distinctly prohibited. As a finale, he slipped in an order forbidding them to covet anything that already belonged to somebody else, but he didn't actually think this one had much of a chance.

Moses spent quite a while on the mount, while The Lord laid out a lot of other laws for the Hebrews to follow. For example, he was extremely particular in describing how he wished to be worshipped at that time, with his taste tending distinctly toward the sacrifice of innocent animals of various well-defined kinds.

"...and don't think of sending me the inferior, cast-off items that you can't trade elsewhere. I want to see perfect specimens," he warned. "In fact, you might want to think about selling suitable beasts right at the place of sacrifice. Otherwise, there's no telling what kind of crap people will try sending along."

"Oh, one thing more," added The Lord, capriciously, "you Hebrew men...you mustn't round the corners of your heads or mar the corners of your beards."

"I beg your pardon?" asked Moses.

"You heard me."

"But...I don't understand."

"Not my problem. Figure it out."

"Could you be just a little more explicit?"

"I don't think so."

It may be that God was checking to make sure Moses was listening carefully, or he may have been merely pulling his leg with this cryptic command—to relieve the tension, as it were. But Moses, already straining to remember all the laws, was in no mood to jest, so he just memorized this along with all the rest and the Hebrews were left to interpret it as best they could. They eventually hit on an arrangement of lengthy curls which appeared to fit the bill but left bald men at a distinct disadvantage.

Zipporah had warned Moses to carry a spare tablet and some writing equipment with him in order to take notes, but he didn't like to carry stuff in his pockets, so of course he didn't listen. He was up on the mount for such a long time trying to memorize all the additional laws God had neglected to append to the list that the people lost faith that he would ever return. They became so very unruly that Aaron collected all the gold jewellery they'd brought out of Egypt, melted it down and shaped it into a golden calf, hoping that the worship of this image might distract them for a while. It was a great success: their excess energy was successfully diverted to feasting and singing and dancing, and Aaron told them they could get naked, too, although it's hard to see how that could have been expected to make things more orderly.

When Moses finally arrived, he was so frustrated to see the people already breaking who knows how many of God's new commandments that he threw down the tablets in a rage, smashing them to bits. It did not put him into a better humour to realize that he now had to climb back up the mountain and beg God to scratch out another couple of tablets to replace the broken ones. Irritated, he ordered a few thousand of the rowdiest revellers killed, then trudged back up the mountain, trying to think up a plausible explanation that would get all the rest of them off the hook.

Sure enough, God had heard rumours about the golden calf and was outraged. "They've broken my most favourite commandment!" thundered The Lord. "I'll kill them all!" He was very hot-tempered in those days.

"Wait," begged Moses. "I hadn't had a chance yet to read them the bit about worshipping no graven images. How could they know? You see, I...um...tripped on the way down and smashed the tablets...by mistake."

"You couldn't have just *told* them?" snapped The Lord. "The tablets were merely meant to be a memory aid, for Heaven's sake."

Moses fibbed that he had been trying so hard to memorize the lesser laws that he must have neglected to give enough attention to the Big Ten, and had forgotten some of them. God began to wonder whether he'd chosen the right person for the job, but he forgave Moses and whipped up a fresh set of tablets, although he didn't have time to make them nearly as fancy as the first ones.

"You'd better be a whole lot more careful this time," he warned, "because my fingernails are getting all chipped from the calligraphy, and I don't intend to do this again. Ever."

Moses promised he'd take care, and scrambled back down the mountain before God could change his mind. When the people learned how Moses had covered for them, they were so appreciative that they promised to cherish the tablets forever, and they conscientiously obeyed every single one of the commandments for well over a week.

Struggling to conquer growing doubts about the worthiness of at least some of his chosen people, The Lord nevertheless maintained his determination to lead the Hebrews to their designated homeland.

Chapter 4

The Wilderness

As time and miles went by and the pleasures of hiking in the wilderness grew rather stale, the people began to get peevish, and they became very hard to please. The sun was too bright, the air was too dry, their luggage was too heavy, and their feet were beginning to blister.

When their meagre store of grain had run out, God surprised them with a daily rain of manna, which filled their empty bellies and tasted like wafers made with honey. Once they learned to cover their heads so it wouldn't get stuck in their hair, they simply had to gather it every morning, brush off the sand, and their culinary problems were solved. They were grateful...for a while. (The women were grateful for longer. It gave them a break from cooking—much like take-out, only closer.)

As they began to get bored with this constant, unrelieved diet of manna, they began to remember fondly the food they had been accustomed to eat in Egypt. It hadn't been remarkable in any way, as they were slaves, you'll remember, but nostalgia improved it significantly in flavour and variety, and they saw no reason why The Lord couldn't be just a little more lavish and provide some diversity.

They craved meat—or, at very least, fish—although the more level-headed among them admitted that the chances of fish materializing in the wilderness seemed slim. Eventually, they became obsessed with this desire; it filled their dreams and monopolized their conversation. In fact, they so whined and complained about it that Moses began to feel like a harried father caring for three hundred thousand fretful babies...which was too many altogether. Finally God became irritated by their interminable whimpering.

"Meat you want, and meat you shall have," snapped The Lord. "I'll give you meat aplenty...and you'll eat it until it spurts out of your noses!" The Lord hates ingratitude.

Forthwith, he caused a strong wind to blow inland from the sea, driving innumerable plump quails into the wilderness where they fell, hip deep, around the camp. Aware that the delicious birds would eventually rot, the people scrambled to gather every last one, and stuffed themselves until they vomited—then they ate again.

As the meat passed its prime and became tainted, the thousands who continued to gorge sickened, and God allowed many of them to die...just to teach them a lesson in greed control. This didn't work in any long term sense, but at least it put an end to culinary criticism for a while.

When they approached Canaan, which was the place The Lord had selected to be their homeland, Moses sent the tribal leaders as spies, to preview the land. When they returned, they brought back a tempting selection of delicious fruits.

"You should see! Farms, orchards, vineyards...it's a land of milk and honey. Well, okay, that's maybe an exaggeration, but for sure a land of grapes and pomegranates and figs."

However, it was not all good news. They had expected to simply sashay in and make themselves at home, but they began to suspect that the residents of this rich land might not leave without a struggle.

"Sure...there's plenty of housing for all of us, but they'd have to agree to give it up because we would never be able to take it from them. The cities are way too strong...we can't be expected to attack such strong cities! And the men...they must be descended from giants. They're huge!

"You know, all things considered, maybe it would be wiser to move along and find some other place to settle. Someplace easier."

Before long, they had convinced the people that The Lord had probably cooked up this whole 'promised land' thing as a cruel practical joke designed to lead the Hebrews to their destruction. They got ready to select a new leader and rush back to their brick-making jobs in Egypt before the positions were all filled.

Only Caleb and Joshua among the leaders sensed that it might seem ungracious to turn their backs on God's gift so unceremoniously. "We should at least *try* to conquer the inhabitants and take possession of the land," they insisted. "It isn't quite as convenient as if the country was handed to us on a platter, perhaps, but it would at least save us the long, dusty hike back to Egypt."

Disgusted at the Hebrews' willingness to return to bondage after he'd gone to so much trouble to spring them, The Lord devised a suitable punishment:

"All those who fled Egypt...the ones who've been doing all the griping—they'll die griping in the wilderness; they'll *never* get the land I promised them. But Caleb and Joshua...they were willing to fight for it, and they deserve to have it. But not just yet."

So he shooed them all back towards the Red Sea, to wander in the desert for a few more decades, giving them plenty of time to meditate on the error of their ways and work on their obedience skills.

Life wandering in the wilderness was no picnic, but when water ran out entirely, things began to look really grim. Moses, always ready to try an inventive solution, hit a rock with a stick. He didn't expect great results from this approach, so he had to scramble out of the way to avoid wetting his robe when a stream flowed out. He composed his face to look like he knew it all along and nonchalantly gave thanks to The Lord, who told him not to count on it happening too often.

The people were grateful...for the time it took to drink. Unfortunately, having quenched their thirst, they were free to focus their attention again on their stomachs. You'd think the Hebrews might have learned by now that God had little sympathy for criticism of the limited menu. Well, they were nothing if not persistent, and they began to complain yet again that they were sick of eating manna day in and day out. Suspecting that they might not fall for the putrid bird ploy this time, God sent fiery serpents to bite them. A lot of them died—again—and the rest took the hint and shut up about the food for the remainder of the trek. Moses, cleverly fashioning a serpent out of brass, perched it up on a pole. Whoever was bitten had only to look at this brass serpent, and they would recover.

"But...isn't that a graven image?" asked the people.

"I suppose...so what?"

"Well, we're not supposed to worship graven images. You said."

"You're not worshipping. You're merely...looking. It's altogether different."

"How is it different?"

"I can't exactly explain. It's subtle."

"Well, it looks a lot like a graven image."

"Look, do you want to be cured, or what?"

"Well, sure. But it's just that..."

"Oh, go away and leave me alone." He was getting too old for this kind of thing.

At first, when they found that they were denied passage through inhabited lands, the Hebrews avoided confrontation by prudently skirting these areas. But as they grew in strength and numbers, they began to fight those who would not allow them to pass through peaceably. As they had God on their side, they invariably won these battles, whereupon they took possession of the lands and slaughtered the inhabitants, sparing only the virgins for their own personal use. Of course, they were careful to purify the girls before using them, lest the Hebrew men be defiled. No doubt the maidens felt highly honoured to be made use of by such fastidious men.

When they reached Moab, near Jericho, the King of the Moabites worried that his country would be overrun in turn, so he summoned Balaam the seer, offering him honours and rewards to put a curse on the Hebrews so that they could be driven away. After much coy hesitation—possibly designed to drive his price up—Balaam agreed to meet with the king but he made no promises, for he'd heard that the Hebrews had been blessed by a very powerful god.

Balaam climbed on his ass and set out for Moab, but the ass startled him with an assortment of uncharacteristic antics, bolting off the path, squashing up against a wall—crushing Balaam's foot in the process—and most inconveniently falling down flat on the ground under him.

Balaam's beatings elicited an unexpected response from the ass. "Hey, don't blame me! An angel made me do it," she said.

"An angel," scoffed Balaam. "I doubt it."

"An angel of God. He wouldn't let me pass."

"Right. Why?"

"Maybe the road is closed for construction further on...how should I know?"

As Balaam was preparing to beat her senseless, The Lord, chuckling, confessed to the prank and allowed Balaam to proceed.

When he arrived at the city in Moab and tried, at the king's request, to curse the Hebrews, the only words God allowed him to speak sounded suspiciously like praise.

He tried a change of location and a fresh sacrificial offering for his curse. "The mighty Hebrew army will be as a ravening lion feeding on its prey and lapping the blood of the slain," he wheezed.

This was still not very comforting to the Moabites. He tried yet another venue and yet more impressive offerings.

The message there was no more encouraging. "The victorious Hebrew people will devour their enemies ...crushing their bones and piercing them through with arrows," he choked.

The king of Moab was understandably dissatisfied with the results of this abortive curse-fest. Even the most talented of his public relations people would have difficulty using these revelations to bolster the morale of his army.

"Big help *you* were! About the honours we discussed? The rewards?" growled the king, "Forget it! And if you're looking for a letter of reference...look elsewhere." He sourly ordered Balaam to return home. This was fine with Balaam, who no longer anticipated any great and prosperous future for anyone who opposed the Hebrews.

After 40 years passed, God was ready to allow the Hebrews to cross the Jordan River into Canaan. All of the original tribal leaders who'd escaped out of Egypt had died on the trip except Moses, and he could hardly contain his excitement at the prospect of entering the new homeland. He mentioned this to The Lord.

"Sorry," said The Lord. "You can't go."

"What do you *mean* I can't go? I've been looking forward to this for forty years!" Moses was a bit shrill, but he was really upset.

"I vowed that none of you old-timers would live to enter the promised land. You remember..."

"But I've worked so *hard*. And I've been good ...haven't I been good? I'm your favourite!"

"Well, yes."

"You couldn't possibly have meant *me!*"

"Actually, no. But I forgot to make an exception for you, at the time. It was an unfortunate oversight, but I can't very well go back on my word now—it would be undignified."

So Moses was permitted just one quick glance at the rich land across the river before he expired—he was one hundred and twenty years old at the time—leaving Joshua to take his place and lead the people across to claim their prize.

Fortunately, though, before he died he was able to recap for the Hebrews the laws God had discussed with him on the mount, adding a few that he had forgotten to mention at the time.

Some of those laws were quite durable, and helped the people to live decent lives: they were instructed to give to the poor, treat their neighbours as they treated themselves, and be kind to strangers, for they had been strangers themselves, often enough. The Lord emphasized the difference between those who sin through ignorance and would be forgiven, and those who ignored his commandments and sinned intentionally. For these latter, the punishment was to be as severe as the crime: a life for a life, an eye for an eye, a tooth for a tooth. Clearly, in those days God favoured a direct approach to crime control. The penalties were designed to discourage indulgence in violent behaviour...through the judicious employment of fear. They also had the useful corollary effect of reducing repeat offences in a very physical sense. A toothless bully could still push people around, it's true, but a one-eyed man had leeway for only one more eye-related offence before he put himself at a distinct disadvantage.

Other laws were very specific. For example, it was expressly forbidden to misdirect the blind. Apparently enough people found this an amusing pastime that God felt he had to put a stop to it. And in a fight between two men, their wives were not allowed to step in and grab the testicles of the opponent—not even for a joke. The offending hand would be cut off, which helped to ensure that it wouldn't become a habit.

"If you fail to obey these laws," Moses thundered, "God will curse you with everything from fever and burning and sword to mildew..."

"Mildew?" muttered a woman toward the back of the crowd. "Can people even *get* mildew?"

"Hey, don't tempt him," whispered her neighbour.

"Maybe he meant athlete's foot."

"I think we're missing the point. Be quiet and listen."

Moses was still listing curses: "...and scabs and itches and madness and blindness..."

"I still think that mildew thing is a mistake," the woman went on. "He's getting pretty old...maybe he forgot what God actually said...or maybe he heard it wrong."

"Shut up and listen," snapped her companion.

"But it's important. What did The Lord actually threaten? Maybe it was something worse!"

"...and new varieties of plague that last a really long time," Moses finished, and turned to leave.

"Hey!" shouted the woman. "Are you very sure about the mildew?"

Moses stopped, and glowered "Look, if you just do what you're *told*, you won't have to worry about it." He walked away, muttering, "People give me a pain."

But Moses wasn't kidding himself. He knew very well that as soon as they got everything The Lord could be persuaded to give them, the people were going to turn right around and break the laws anyway. So he wrote a song to remind them forever, whenever they were punished for transgressions, that he had told them so.

Chapter 5

Joshua

It was clear to Joshua that such a large group of people as he was leading had no hope of sauntering into the land of Canaan unnoticed, and he was not nearly naïve enough to expect that the Canaanites would relinquish their land graciously. In preparation for an attack on the walled city of Jericho, he sent two of his soldiers into the city as spies. Somehow—it might have been by mere coincidence—they found their way to the home of the harlot Rahab. It appears that they found her particular vicinity sufficiently intriguing—from a tactical standpoint, no doubt—that they were compelled to take lodgings in her home; they stayed so long, in fact, that the king of Jericho heard they were there and peevishly sent his soldiers to capture them. Rahab had heard enough from the idle pillow chatter of her two visitors to know that a battle was imminent, and she had no intention of leaving her fate to the mercy of gods or men.

Hustling the two Israelites up onto the roof, she ensured that they were well hidden under some spare stalks of flax that were being stored there in preparation for spinning—she was a woman of many talents—and ran back down to meet the soldiers.

"Sorry to keep you waiting, fellows. I had to make myself decent," she teased, raising her eyebrow in a saucily meaningful manner. What can I do for *you* today?"

"We're searching for two Israelites. We heard they were here with you."

"Well, my lads, you may be right. I did, indeed have two guests...paying companions, if you know what I mean." She saw that they did. "But as to their origin...I don't tend to inquire too particularly, you understand. They left just a short while ago. Feel free to look around, if you like." She held the door open welcomingly.

The men stepped through the door.

"Of course," she added, quickly, "you might want to step lively. They were heading toward the river." They hesitated. "The gate will be closing soon, but they can't have gotten far," she added, knowing full well that they hadn't gone far at all. "If you hurry, you have a fair chance of catching them. And do come back...anytime. Special rates for our brave boys in uniform."

The soldiers were already rushing enthusiastically off toward the river Jordan in search of the two spies, passing out through the city gates just as these were being slammed shut for the night, which effectively prevented any further search of her home, at least until they were reopened in the morning.

Rahab returned to the roof and fished the two Israelites out from under the flax stalks. Her house abutted the town walls, as was typical for someone of her calling—the fastidious Canaanites arranged to locate their whore houses as far from the city center as possible without making them actually inconvenient of access—and this was certainly not the first time she had been called upon to smuggle a client discreetly out of her home.

"Let me get a cord from the back room," she told them. "I can let you down through the window, and you'll be on the outside of the town wall. If you hide in the woods for a few days until the soldiers give up the search and return to the city, you should be able to get back to your own camp with no problem."

The two young men thanked her profusely and were eager to get started, but Rahab was not ready to let them go, and they needed her help with the rope in order to have any expectation of a discreet exit.

"Not so fast," said Rahab. "I've heard rumours that you Hebrews have enlisted the help of a powerful god in overrunning the land..."

"Yes...yes...our God. The one and only. He's the best. Look, we have to go now." blurted the men.

"Be that as it may. What's even more disturbing to me," she drawled, "you seem to have an unfriendly habit of killing everyone within the towns you capture."

They began to see where she was heading with this line of discussion. "Well...no...not *everyone* exactly..." they started, hesitantly.

"No," she admitted, "not everyone. Sometimes you spare the young virgins. Now, with my track record, I'm guessing that my chances of passing as one of the lucky virgins are pretty slim. What do you think?"

They had to agree that her chances were not good.

"Then we have a problem." she stated. "But I'm sure we can work something out that will be more mutually beneficial."

While they were still dependent on her help, she elicited a promise from the two spies that she and her family would be spared, in the event of a general populace massacre. The men instructed her to tie a scarlet thread across the window from which they were escaping, and vowed that the people in her home wouldn't be harmed, on condition that she keep silent about their escape and whereabouts. (In fact, they were themselves not keen on Joshua hearing all the particulars of the business that had kept them in her home for so long.)

Having supervised their escape, she then promptly tied scarlet threads across that and every other window in the house, for good measure. This later became her trademark, and an excellent marketing tool it was, until the more eye-catching red lights became fashionable.

Guided by the information gathered by his spies, Joshua decided to lay siege to Jericho, expecting to starve its people into submission. The Hebrew army surrounded the apparently impregnable city walls, allowing no one to leave or to enter, and the inhabitants were prevented from bringing the harvest in from the fields. But as the weeks passed, it became apparent that the townsfolk were more resilient than anticipated, and had prudently stocked their store-houses with enough excess grain from last year's crop to cover just such a contingency. They remained snug within their walls, and as the Children of Israel were still on the outside, looking in, God suggested another plan.

"Every day for six days," instructed God, "seven priests are to walk around the city bearing the holy writings in a casket, each blowing a blast on a ram's horn trumpet."

"You're kidding," protested Joshua. "What possible good can that do?"

"Seven priests," insisted The Lord. "Blowing trumpets. Just do it."

It sounded a bit thin, but The Lord had a good track record, so Joshua agreed to give it a try.

So they did. Unfortunately, nothing was achieved beyond bringing a few of the cheekier townspeople to the top of the walls to point and laugh.

When The Lord stopped by at the end of the sixth day and saw the city still intact, he addressed the disheartened Hebrews. "Don't think of blaming *me*," he said. "It should have worked. You have one day left. Throw some enthusiasm into it this time."

So on the seventh day, the priests rose at daybreak and scampered around the city seven times. Then they blew a blast on all of their trumpets at once and every Hebrew shouted at the top of his or her lungs, just for good measure. It created a terrible din and the walls of Jericho came tumbling down, exactly as God had predicted, allowing the soldiers to enter with ease. (Oddly enough, the Hebrews never attempted to use this effective tactic again, no matter how many cities they attacked. Maybe it was simply too embarrassing.)

As usual, the inhabitants of the city were all massacred except, of course, for Rahab and her family, for Joshua was a man more honourable than most and he kept his soldiers' promise. The city was burnt to the ground, but Rahab phlegmatically relocated her family to live among the people of Israel, where she recognized a ground floor opportunity to build up a thriving whorehouse franchise in the fledgling state.

Before long, the Israelites had a firmly established reputation for fighting and winning; also for killing, burning and raping. When the women of Gibeon learned that their city would be, in all probability, on the hit list, they felt that an innovative strategy was required.

"We can't fight these brutes," they stated. "We need to make terms with them *before* they invade the town."

"Out of the question!" exclaimed the men. "All the other guys are fighting...we want to fight too. Our honour *requires* it."

"You'd put your families at risk?" challenged the outspoken wife of one of the town elders.

"Certainly. Our honour..."

"Don't be fools! The Israelites were able to deploy an army of thirty-five thousand against the town of Ai, and there may be more where those came from. You're no match for them on your *best* day. We're not going to stand by and let our city be razed to the ground to satisfy *your* sorry sense of honour. Everything we cherish will be destroyed and we'll all be massacred. Forget it!"

"And another thing," added a pretty young matron, "*we* don't fancy being picked over like day-old fruit in the marketplace by a bunch of randy Israelite soldiers. Is that what you want?" She glared at her crestfallen husband. "Honour indeed!" she spat in disgust.

Finally, seeing the wisdom of their advice, the men agreed to carry out a plan that might improve their bargaining position. Dressed in old, tattered clothing and footwear and carrying a meagre store of dry, mouldy bread and dusty, woefully empty wine skins on their most worn-out asses, a few of the townsmen rode over to Joshua's camp. Claiming to be ambassadors from a distant country, they requested that a treaty of peace be negotiated.

"I don't know..." said Joshua, to his lieutenant, "I've been kind of busy, with all the death and destruction and all. I haven't had a chance to take a good look at the map. Where is Gibeon located? I have no idea. Is it close? If it's too close..."

His lieutenant shrugged his shoulders. He didn't know either.

But the ambassadors pointed out the condition of their gear. "Look," they said, "we're ambassadors. You don't think we set out looking like this, do you? When we left home, we looked really spiffy. We were fully provisioned, with hot, fresh bread and full wine skins. But it's been a long journey, so we simply want to make a deal, and get back home to our wives."

Joshua saw the logic in this and, considering such apparently distant neighbours to be no great threat, he made a treaty agreeing to spare the city of Gibeon and its adjacent towns. In return, the Gibeonites would serve the Israelites in whatever ways Joshua required. (This may seem a little open-ended, but they had never expected to be able to negotiate much of a bargain, and felt lucky just to have avoided death and destruction.)

Three days later, the Israelites, wandering around the neighbourhood, stumbled upon an inconveniently located city. They prepared to attack.

"Not that it matters..." asked the company clerk, "but what's the name of this place? Just for the record, you understand."

The nearest local Canaanite spy responded, cooperatively, "It's the city of Gibeon, sir."

"Gibeon..." mused Joshua. "Isn't that the name that scruffy delegation of ambassadors mentioned the other day?"

"Um...yes," confirmed his lieutenant, "I think it is."

"But it's right in the midst of our new land!"

"It does seem so."

"Didn't they say it was much farther away?"

"Come to think of it, I don't remember that they said exactly *where* it was."

"Somehow I had the impression that it was much farther away. Do you suppose anybody would notice if we go ahead and destroy it anyway?"

"Oh, I don't think *that* matters. But you did swear to a treaty...and I think I remember you mentioning the name of The Lord. He's been known to get rather moody when his name's taken in vain."

All Joshua could do was to call the townsmen a few unflattering names and make them servants, hewing wood and drawing water for the house of God. For their part, the Gibeonites figured it still beat rampant killing and burning, and their women remained as safe as women ever are when there are soldiers in the neighbourhood.

As Joshua and his mighty men of valour proceeded to fight their way across the land, God stuck by them, never hesitating to step in with a storm of deadly hailstones or largish rocks where it seemed necessary in order to win a battle. In this way, the area was cleared of all serious opposition and the Israelites were able to take possession of their long-awaited homeland.

This does, however, leave us in some doubt about the interpretation of God's intention when he ordered, "Thou shalt not kill." He clearly had no aversion to killing in time of war; in fact he enthusiastically encouraged and abetted it. Neither, judging by the amount of looting involved in these exercises, was killing for gain completely out of bounds. In fact, the Israelites now, with God's blessing, lived in cities which they had not built and ate from vines which they had not planted. Perhaps The Lord had meant this particular commandment to apply only after his chosen people had made themselves comfortable. Or maybe there had been an exemption for wartime which Moses forgot to mention, in all the confusion about the broken tablets on the mount.

In any case, the Israelites buried Abraham's bones, which they had considerately carted along with them all this time, and settled down to enjoy their new homes. They prudently kept pretty much to themselves, fearing that intermarriage with the native peoples might smudge their faith and tempt them to waste their time and offend The Lord by trying out other, less partisan gods. And any former inhabitants who had not been slaughtered or driven away became second-class citizens, barely tolerated and forced to scratch out a living as best they could.

Chapter 6

The Judges

Try as they might, the children of Israel continually went astray, breaking The Lord's commandments in a wide variety of creative ways. They especially had trouble with the one forbidding them to test-run other gods, for they were an inquisitive people, and every time they heard about an unfamiliar god, they just had to check it out. Their true God would jealously withdraw his favour, and they would immediately find themselves invaded by one or more of the defeated Canaanite enemies who were still hanging around on the sidelines waiting for a chance to get back in the game. During these times of trouble The Lord would send an Israelite from among them—a 'judge'—to win a battle or two if necessary, and set God's Chosen back on the right path. (They didn't really do much judging, as a rule, which makes the title rather a puzzling choice. But then, maybe judging wasn't always what was needed.)

The people would thereafter obey the judge devotedly and enthusiastically, but sadly, judges didn't live forever, and when each died, the people lost no time reverting to their headstrong ways.

As time went by, the Israelites found it considerably more profitable to exact tribute from the conquered peoples than to drive them away. They always came back again anyway, with weapons and an attitude, so it was more effective to leave them where they could be supervised. Over the years—because it was a violent age—the Israelites were occasionally themselves overcome and subjugated for short periods by some stronger nation, but they always managed to shake themselves loose...with The Lord's help, of course.

The judges, on their part, were not simply assembly-line heroes sent by God to save the day. Oh, no, they were raised from the people, each vigorously bringing his own unique talents to bear. There was, for example, the peerless soldier who single-handedly skewered six hundred Philistines with a humble ox-goad. (This number may have been a little inflated in the heat of the battle, but it was definitely not less than sixteen or seventeen Philistines...and they were big ones.) And the courageous diplomat who jammed a concealed dagger into the fat gut of the king of Moab in his own parlour after sharing confidences, then, locking the doors behind him to delay detection, fled fearlessly out the back way and off into the night. After a parade of these mental and moral giants, the children of Israel were indeed past due for a leader with some understanding.

Imagine their surprise when this turned out to be a maiden named Deborah—the first true judge of Israel! Now, the patriarchs had never been remarkable for elevating their women to positions of power, but the children of Israel were a shrewd people and were able to recognize excellence, if only it leaped out and bit them in the ass.

Deborah's passionate devotion to justice was combined with sensitive insight into human nature, giving her a unique ability to pry the true meaning and intention of God's laws loose from the cumbersome incrustation of patriarchal interpretation. The people soon realized that Deborah's guidance was sound, and would relieve them of the necessity to consciously think for themselves just as effectively as the countless patriarchal mini-laws did...and less oppressively. Soon, she could not relax in the shade beneath her favourite palm tree without her garden filling with individuals seeking advice or demanding that she resolve disputes. Eventually she had to request that they form orderly lines and, when there was a crowd, she was forced to insist that they each take a number and await their turns patiently.

As her reputation for justice and wisdom spread and prominent visitors from far and wide sought her out, their concerns and confidences gave her a unique opportunity to evaluate the problems besetting her country. The king of Canaan had been threatening their land and harassing their people for twenty years, and now Sisera, a brave and powerful general, had risen up to lead the Canaanites. The loyalty of the troops who followed him was absolute, and there was an imminent danger that the land of Israel would be completely crushed. It was a critically dangerous situation, so she decided to abandon all pretence of womanly modesty and take pre-emptive action.

When she sent for Barak, who was considered the strongest military leader at that time among the Israelites, she was held in such high regard that even this battle-hardened veteran thought it best to come immediately. Fortunately it was a slow day, and he only had to wait in line for about fifteen minutes before she was able to see him.

"I must apologize for the delay," said Deborah. "Thanks for being so patient. I know you're a busy man these days.

"I'll get right to the point. The situation of Israel is very grave. I urge you to take ten thousand men immediately to the river Kishon, where they can use the terrain to advantage and attack the Canaanite army with full force. I'm convinced that only a total victory will make our land safe again."

"Right. Do you have any particular ten thousand men in mind?" asked Barak, sarcastically.

"No." responded Deborah, with equanimity. "Any ten thousand men of your choice would be quite fine, I'm sure."

Barak wasn't eager to risk his troops on the untried military judgment of this woman. In fact, he was concerned about the reputation of Sisera, and not at all sure that he could prevail against such a passionately devoted military force.

Hoping to avoid the issue, he offered her a challenge. "You surely can't expect me to commit my troops to this action based on your personal opinion unless, of course, you're prepared to accompany the army yourself." He sat back with a smirk, and waited.

"Of course not," she agreed. "If you'll simply take a turn around the garden while I get a few things together, I'll be ready to leave with you in a jiffy."

The shock of her response erased the smug smile from his face.

Weighing the determination that the valour of this woman might inspire in his soldiers, Barak decided to give it a shot. He'd take a win any way he could get it. And if The Lord struck her dead for her presumption...well, that was *her* problem.

So Deborah strode to centre stage. Ignoring the discomfort of battle, she played her part bravely, shaming even the most hesitant of soldiers into the semblance of courage and ensuring a victory, which would have to be forever credited to the leadership of...a woman.

And yet, God did not strike her dead. In fact, he seemed to be sitting right up front, enjoying the show!

Although the Canaanite force had been effectively destroyed, the leader Sisera escaped on foot. He knew that he alone commanded enough loyalty to assemble yet another army throw against the Israelites, so he overcame his pride and ran like a jackrabbit to save his skin. By the time he came upon the home of a woman named Jael, in the countryside and away from any town, he was exhausted. As he was aware that her husband was presently on peaceful terms with the Canaanite king, Sisera did not hesitate to approach the tent, drooping with weariness.

"I need some rest," he grunted at Jael. He was much too tired to be tactful. "And keep on watch while I sleep. Find a way to side-track anyone who comes looking for me." He stumbled in and threw himself on her bed—muddy boots and all.

This turned out to be a bad day for Sisera all round, for Jael's husband was away from home, and she had ideas of her own about this war. Nevertheless, with every appearance of compliance, she made him comfortable.

"Bring me a cup of cold water," he demanded, rudely.

"Oh, I can't permit you to shock your system with water," she protested. "It may do you harm. I have fresh goat's milk. It will be much more nourishing, and it's delicious. I must insist."

"Whatever. Just bring it now and stop prattling."

The goat's milk much more effectively hid her addition of soothing, sedative herbs which, unknowing, he drank down in a refreshing gulp. Sitting down for a moment, Jael listened to him snore and considered her options.

She believed the welfare of the Israelites required that he be dead. Unaware that his army had been destroyed—he hadn't troubled to mention this when he dropped in—she feared the imminent arrival of a rescue crew...so she needed him to be dead, *fast.* Her husband, fearing for his own safety on the road, had taken all of his weapons with him, leaving her with nothing much to work with (and, incidentally, with no means of protection. She took a moment to appreciate his thoughtfulness.) Time was short—resources were limited—and her eye fell on the tent-peg. A kitchen knife would have been easier, of course, but the tent-peg would make a much more dramatic statement. So fetching a largish hammer, gently positioning the tent peg at the sleeping man's temple and frowning with distaste, she threw her full weight into the swing and nailed him securely to the bed. Naturally, he died. Cleaning up the worst of the mess, she changed into a fresh robe, and sat outside the tent, awaiting Barak's arrival with the pursuit team. The whole incident had been most unpleasant, but quite necessary.

Deborah was quick to see the poetry in the situation—a woman's decisive action had led the victory and another's brave and bloody act had prevented further threat to the nation. So, being a person of many talents, she sat right down and wrote a rousing song to make sure nobody ever forgot it.

The Canaanite soldiers certainly remembered it for a good long while. It was some time before even the most depraved of them could enjoy fancies of raping the daughters of Israel. The very idea gave them a headache.

The children of Israel enjoyed peace for another forty years before the Midianites poured into the land like a swarm of locusts, destroying many of the crops and eating up most of what was left. When The Lord searched for the Israelite Gideon to appoint him commander and offer help in driving the enemy out, he found that mighty man of valour hiding in his farmyard, behind a winepress. Creeping out, Gideon reluctantly gathered together a huge army, but he wanted to be sure that God would be with them.

"Lord," he called, "I need to know that you'll be fighting on our side. Give me a sign. Nothing fancy—a smallish miracle would do."

He waited.

"Lord," he ventured again, "I don't want to press you, but it has occurred to me that you might be too busy to think up something suitably insignificant—I don't want to trouble you for one of your flashy, impressive miracles—I'm just a simple farmer. How about this: I'll go into battle right away if only you arrange that this pile of fleece in the yard is dew-soaked in the morning, while the ground around it remains dry."

To his chagrin, in the morning the pile of soaking wet fleece sat waiting on the dry ground.

Wringing it out, Gideon addressed God one last time. "I don't mean to be difficult," he said, "but perhaps the little miracle I devised may be a tad equivocal. I mean, a prankster with a watering can might have...anyway, I'll be *sure* you're with us if the fleece is dry tomorrow, and all the *ground* is wet."

The next morning, he slogged through the muddy yard, picked up the bone-dry fleece that lay there and prepared for battle, consoling himself that his thirty-two thousand troops should be able to mop up even the mighty Midianite army without too much trouble.

But when they faced the Midianites, God decided that there were too many soldiers fighting with Gideon. People might think the children of Israel won through sheer force of numbers and give The Lord no credit at all for the victory.

He found Gideon standing atop a hill, confidently reviewing his troops. They filled the plain surrounding him, weapons flashing in a most comforting manner.

"Gideon," God demanded, "I want you to tell the soldiers that anyone who is afraid can leave."

Gideon's face fell. "But...anyone...?" he stammered.

"Anyone," insisted The Lord. "Now."

Gideon made the announcement, and twenty-two thousand men promptly set off for home, at a trot. There were still a lot of soldiers standing around on the plain, but they had plenty of elbow room now. Gideon's comfort level dipped accordingly.

God reviewed the revised army, and decided there were still too many. "You're going to have to get rid of more," he insisted.

Gideon panicked. "But these remaining men have all shown themselves to be loyal, willing soldiers," he pointed out. "How can I choose some and reject the rest? They'd be insulted," he pleaded, hopefully.

But The Lord was ready with what he decided was a fair plan. "Bring all the men down to the river to refresh themselves," he demanded. "The ones who kneel to drink are to be sent away. The ones who lap the water from their hands—those will become your army." Unhappily for Gideon, there were only three hundred hand-lappers. He was going to have to rely on formulating a really creative battle plan.

Dividing his men into three companies, he issued each man a trumpet and a pitcher with a lamp inside. They snuck down and surrounded the enemy camp; then, at a pre-arranged signal from Gideon, they all smashed their pitchers, held up the lamps in a threatening manner and blew their trumpets savagely. For some reason which may be more obvious to you than it is to me, this caused the Midianites to start fighting fiercely among themselves, decimating their numbers significantly. The survivors fled with Gideon's men in hot pursuit, slaughtering every man they were lucky enough to catch.

It was a great success. The Lord got the credit, the people toed the line, and the land was at peace for yet another forty years.

Judge succeeded judge, every one bringing the Israelites back to the worship of The Lord...for a while. But with the death of each, the people always turned to other, more flamboyant gods who countenanced much rowdier behaviour. Nevertheless, whenever their wayward ways resulted in invasion and oppression by outside forces, the Israelites expected God to step in and save the day. More than a little fed up with their fickleness, The Lord suggested that they go whine to their fun gods for help against their enemies, and see how far that would take them. His patience was wearing thin, and he threatened to cut off his special emergency aid program if he didn't see a bit more loyalty sometime soon.

The judges themselves were not above trying to bribe God when they felt it might encourage him to continue his support. Jephtha, for example, rashly vowed—in return for The Lord's aid in defeating the Philistines and the children of Ammon—to offer up as a burnt offering whatever should come out of his doors to meet him on his return from battle. The battle was won and Jephtha returned home to be greeted eagerly by his young daughter, running out to honour him with an innocent little victory dance. Chagrined, he chided her for causing him this sorrow, for now he would have to sacrifice her, like any ox or lamb, to repay The Lord for his help.

(It's difficult to guess who he'd thought *would* be first through that door, as he had no other children and the dog wasn't allowed in the house. Perhaps he was hoping it would have been his wife.)

The girl was not entirely pleased about it either, but a promise is a promise and her father was quite insistent, so she decided to make the best of a bad situation. "Surely," she pleaded, "if I am to be denied the delight of bearing children and serving a husband for the rest of my life, I can at least be allowed a short retreat in the mountains to lament my virginity with a few companions."

Her father—perhaps feeling just a teeny bit guilty that she was to die for his vow while he had risked nothing at all—agreed that this did not seem an altogether unreasonable request. Choosing a few very 'special friends', she set out to enjoy an extended Bon Voyage party in the mountains, and weeks stretched into months as her companions found creative ways to console her for her misfortune.

After she had enjoyed as much consolation as she thought she could get away with, she returned home to face her fate.

"Well," snapped Jephtha, "you certainly took long enough. You're lucky God hasn't become impatient. He might have punished *me.*"

"I'm sorry," she replied, "it has been rather a long time, hasn't it? Well, time flies when you're having fun."

He glared at her suspiciously. "You'd better be just as virginal as you were when you left," he warned. "I can't present The Lord with damaged goods, you know. It would make a bad impression."

"How can you even ask? I'm as unsullied as your own heart. Why, my friends and I spent the entire time thinking only of how the purity of your sacrifice would impress The Lord. We thought of it day and night. I'm still thinking about it now." She smiled.

Something in that smile was not reassuring. But guessing that God might frown on any last minute substitutions, he chose to believe that she was still a suitably unblemished offering and the sacrifice proceeded as originally planned.

After several additional judges had come and gone and the Philistines had once again conquered Israel, an uncommonly strong young Israelite named Samson found himself attracted to a pretty Philistine woman. Mixed marriages were never a popular choice among his people, but his brawn had always intimidated others into giving him his own way, which made him rather headstrong. He was he was determined to marry the bride of his choice and would brook no interference. As he traveled to court her, carrying with him nothing but a fistful of posies, he was attacked by a mangy lion, desperate from starvation. After ripping the beast apart with his bare hands, he washed away the gore in a wayside stream, made himself presentable and proceeded on his way. The Philistine beauty, overlooking the battered state of the flowers, subsequently accepted his proposal of marriage.

On returning for the wedding, he couldn't resist the temptation to revisit the scene of his triumph over the lion, just to have a glance at the remains and gloat a bit. He was surprised to find the skin unaccountably buzzing with bees and filled with honey, but he was not a man of deep thought and symbolism was not at all in his line. He simply grabbed an impromptu snack at the site and proceeded to his nuptials. There he slapped together a sly scheme, in an attempt to provide an impressive trousseau for his new wife.

He chose the optimum point in his bachelor party—after his thirty Philistine groomsmen had gotten drunk as fools but before the arrival of the dancing girls—to propose a friendly wager. "How are you Philistines at riddles?" he bellowed. "Do you like a challenge?"

"We're up f'r anythin'," slurred the groomsmen.

"Well, I have a good one for you. And to make it interesting...I'll bet each of you a full set of bed linen and a closet full of clothes that you can't solve it."

"Bring it on!"

Samson struck a suitably histrionic pose. "Out of the eater came forth meat and out of the strong came forth sweetness," he intoned.

It was hardly a fair contest, for they had no way of knowing about Samson's unusual experience, so he seemed certain to win the wager. In fact, he had already begun to calculate the alterations that would be necessary to adjust the largest of their suits to his massive frame.

Unfortunately, he couldn't resist bragging to his bride about his prowess in defeating the lion. Disgusted with him for spoiling the occasion with a childish, crooked wager and suspecting this might indicate an unattractive inclination toward stinginess in his character, she related the story to the groomsmen, who used the information to solve the riddle. Samson, now obliged to steal linens and garments from thirty total strangers in order to pay off the bet, knew that the clue to the riddle could only have come from one source—his new spouse. In a rage, he stomped out and left her, returning to his home empty-handed and alone.

After indulging himself in a good long sulk, he swaggered back to reclaim his wife only to find that she had left her father's house. His angry inquiries elicited only an uncomfortable silence on the part of the townsfolk, but he was finally directed to a stylish dwelling on a side street nearby. The bride he had deserted greeted him at the door with considerably less reticence.

"How dare you come traipsing back here, expecting me to be ready and waiting? You stormed out as though you didn't want me any more, and god knows I could live without *you*. I couldn't see returning all the wedding gifts, so I married the best man the very next day.

"I can't imagine what I saw in you anyway. He's my countryman, and a *much* more suitable match. Besides," she taunted, "he was irresistible in the spiffy new garments he won from you—and he came with a fresh set of bed linens!"

Our hero was not a man to let such a humiliation go unpunished. In a burst of creative inspiration, he tied firebrands to the tails of three hundred foxes and let them loose in the corn fields, which burned to the ground. Following his cue, the Philistines roasted Samson's wife and her father to death for rashly allowing this hothead to enter their midst.

Even Samson, never sensitive to subtleties, recognized this as a personal affront. Slaughtering the culprits, he fled back to his homeland in Judah, but the Philistines sent a sizable force to haul him back for punishment.

In an attempt to rush the Philistines out of their land before some serious damage was done, Samson's own compatriots set out to capture him and bring him as quickly as possible to Philistine justice. They tracked him down and trussed him up, but Samson broke his bonds and slew one thousand of his captors—give or take a few dozen captors—using the jawbone of an ass which lay conveniently at hand; a weapon, incidentally, which really does seem singularly suited to the user. Incredibly, God chose this bonehead to judge over the Israelites for the next twenty years

Eventually he must have tired of the security of his judicial life for he rashly traveled to Gaza to partake of some light recreation and there fell in love with a beauty named Delilah. She, unfortunately, wasn't so fond of him that she couldn't be bribed by the vindictive Philistine lords to pry from him the secret of his great strength.

Donning her scantiest negligee and splashing on her most alluring perfume, she awaited him in her quarters. When he had satisfied his desires and was likely to be most compliant, she stroked his muscular arms admiringly.

"Superb," she purred. "I can't imagine what it must be to control such strength. Won't you share your power with me? Tell me what it would take to subdue such mighty muscles...it would be so seductive..."

He wasn't so sated that he couldn't see an opportunity to lay the groundwork for future dalliance. But when he confided that he could be bound by green willow withes, she promptly tied him up, using seven such withes just to make sure, and delivered him to the Philistine soldiers who were conveniently hiding in the closet. Samson broke the bonds as if they were thread and roughed up the soldiers a bit, to teach them a lesson.

Chuckling good naturedly at the joke, Delilah said "Okay, very funny. But seriously, now...how *can* your strength be overcome?"

Each night describing a more unlikely ritual than the night before, he pretended to tell her his secret, and each night she followed his instructions, attempting to bind him. Each night the Philistines—hiding now behind a curtain, now under the bed—tried to take him away and each night they received a good trouncing for their troubles. Becoming impatient, Delilah met him one night at the doorway, refusing him entrance. "I don't understand why you don't trust me," she pouted. "If you loved me, you wouldn't keep secrets."

Mesmerized by Delilah's beauty—and seeing no soldiers readily apparent in the room—Samson admitted that his strength was in the hair of his head, which had never been shorn. Without it, he admitted, he would be as weak as any other man. Sweeping her up in his powerful arms, he eagerly carried her to the bed.

Quite convinced by now that he was dumber than dirt, Delilah waited until he fell asleep, softly called out to the Philistines—who had been hiding in the root cellar this time—to shave off his hair, collected her substantial reward and watched with equanimity as they carried him, struggling feebly, away. Gouging out his eyes and binding him securely with brass fetters, they put him to work grinding grain in the prison house. In their hurry to leave the fetid place, they left no special instructions for the prison barbers. They had completely overlooked the obvious fact that his shorn hair would undoubtedly continue to grow in captivity. Delilah would certainly have pointed this out to them if they had paid her just a little more.

The lords of the Philistines began planning a gala to celebrate Samson's capture. But what with redecorating the ballroom and problems with the caterers and one lord then another absent on vacation, years went by and the festivities were continually postponed. Finally the big day arrived, and all the most influential nobility gathered. The master of ceremonies had Samson brought in from the prison house to provide the main attraction, for the people were eager to laugh and jeer at the humbled hero. Even the roof held three thousand fun-loving Philistines, jostling to watch the fun.

When the blind captive was led in, he was placed between the two centre pillars for easy viewing. Unfortunately for the Philistines, those two pillars supported the building—and no one had thought to give Samson a shave and a haircut to spruce him up for the performance. He took one pillar in each hand and, with a mighty heave, literally brought down the house. Samson, of course, was crushed but he enjoyed a brief moment's satisfaction hearing the screams of thousands of Philistines dying in agony before he expired.

As you may have noticed, in all this time there were no kings in Israel. Every man was in the habit of doing pretty much whatever he thought was right—or, at least, whatever he thought he could get away with.

Chapter 7

Ruth

During the days when the judges ruled, famine drove a man named Elimelech to leave his home in Judah, taking his wife, Naomi, and his two sons to dwell in the land of Moab. In time, Elimelech died, and Naomi's two sons took Moabite wives, Ruth and Orpah. This was not a lucky family. About ten years later, both sons also died leaving the aging Naomi with no way to survive in Moab. She decided to return to her homeland; the famine had ended and anyway, things could hardly be worse for her there than they were here.

Realizing that she could only be a burden to them, she encouraged her two daughters-in-law to return to the homes of their parents where they might still find husbands willing to support them. Orpah obediently scurried off, praying that her parents would be able to find some man generous enough to accept a wife who was, after all, only used goods. She wasn't expecting much, but she had to hurry, lest an opportunity be escaping even while she lingered.

But Ruth was determined to stay with Naomi. "You can't get rid of me quite so easily, you know," she teased. "We've always gotten along so well, don't you think? And good companions are hard to find.

"Of course, "she added, "I still think you're wrong about the seasoning for a really good lamb stew...I won't budge on that issue. But it's a small thing, after all, and shouldn't be allowed to come between friends. I'm afraid you're stuck with me." *Besides,* Ruth thought to herself, *who knew when she would get another chance to see a bit of the world?*

"My dear," protested Naomi, "I can't let you waste your life on me. I suppose I could try to attract a new husband,"—she struck a comically alluring pose—"and hope to bear a son to replace the one who's lost to you. But I can hardly expect you to wait around for a boy child to ripen to marriageable age. No, it won't do—it won't do at all!"

Ruth laughed. "Well, perhaps that would be a bit much." But she would not be dissuaded. She quite sensibly felt she would rather continue to live in harmony with Naomi than take a gamble on the odds of finding a congenial man to support her.

"I'm not afraid of hard work," she declared, "and it would be no burden for me to support us both. You know, I've always wondered how it must feel to waltz home at the end of the day and find dinner ready on the table and no dishes to clean. Where you go, I go. And that's the end of it!"

On reaching Naomi's ancestral home of Bethlehem, Ruth took advantage of the tradition allowing the poor to follow after the reapers in the fields, gleaning any grain that had been overlooked. It was tiring work, barely gathering in enough to feed the two women, and she had yet to formulate a workable plan for survival after the harvest ended, but Ruth found that she was enjoying the challenge. She had gone from the protection of her father to the protection of her husband, and being unprotected, for a change, didn't seem like such a very bad thing at all.

As she wandered the fields gathering leftover corn, she happened onto the land of Boaz, a wealthy kinsman of Naomi, who noticed the industrious young woman and kindly instructed his reapers to leave plenty of grain in her path and to refrain from molesting her—which was apparently a favourite diversion for the bored farm workers of that era. In fact, Boaz himself came out into the fields and generously invited Ruth to dine with his own workers, discreetly turning a blind eye when she packed up a bag of leftover bits to take home for Naomi.

When she learned of Ruth's meeting with Boaz, Naomi hatched a rather devious scheme for his seduction. Being a traditional sort of woman, she was quite unable to understanding the joy Ruth had found in independence, and Ruth could hardly offend the older woman by telling her that even Naomi's own son had often been less than a joy to live with. Also, Naomi craved a grandchild...and Ruth could provide a reasonable facsimile.

Feeling the noose tighten again around her neck, Ruth was sorely tempted to cut and run. But she loved Naomi and knew how much she missed having a family around her, so she very reluctantly agreed to do as the older woman wished. She waited until Boaz was sleeping off the wine of a festive celebration amidst his labourers on the threshing floor, then crept in and lay down at his side. Awaking at midnight, he recognized the young woman who had attracted his eye in the fields, and felt it would be unmannerly not to take advantage of this gratuitous opportunity. He gallantly spread his cloak over them both, to gain an illusion of privacy, and murmuring tender words of praise for her virtuous reputation, he enthusiastically proceeded to destroy it.

Before morning dawned, Boaz began to feel belated pangs of conscience and spent a few moments considering the most sensitive way of dealing with their new relationship. "Don't you have somewhere else to be?" he asked, considerately. "I don't want to keep you...gleaning leftover grain must take up a good bit of your time. If you want to just quietly leave, I'm sure no one will feel slighted."

She rearranged her clothes and began picking her way past the other sleepers.

"But wait," he whispered, "I'd like to give you a token of my appreciation. Let's see...um...here!" He began to pour barley into her veil, ignoring her gesture of protest. "No, really...I want you to have it." When it was full, he tied it into a bundle and helped her to heave it onto her shoulder.

As she turned away, she allowed her eyes to fill as Naomi had instructed, and squeezed one tear out to trickle down her cheek. One was all she could manage, but it was enough.

"Oh, no! Don't cry," Boaz squeaked. "People will notice! Please...it'll be all right. You'll be a respectable married woman in no time at all. I promise."

Ruth naturally assumed that he meant...married to *him*. And, indeed, after trying unsuccessfully to interest another of Naomi's kinsmen in marrying the young woman, Boaz was cornered into doing the honourable thing and he wed her himself. Obviously a marriage made in heaven.

She bore a son, Obed, in whom Naomi took great joy (Obed was to become grandfather to the great King

David), and it never occurred to anyone, even for a second, to question whether Ruth was contented with her new life. She was universally envied by all the other wives for her good fortune.

"How did you do it? You grabbed away the best catch in the neighbourhood. You must be deliriously happy."

"Yes, I must be," she agreed, "Boaz is so very... adequate a husband."

"And he's so rich!"

"Oh, yes. He is rich." Ruth knew this should offset his deficiencies in the romance department. After all, she was well taken care of. She had everything she could wish for, and had nary a responsibility beyond serving her husband and son. Yet somehow, try as she would to be suitably grateful, Ruth sometimes found herself remembering how good it had felt to manage her own affairs and often wondered wistfully whether she wouldn't have been happier living on her own.

It would be a long time before women would be free to make that choice.

Chapter 8

The Kings

In a time when men were allowed multiple wives and child-bearing was considered woman's only significant achievement, rivalries were bound to flare as women jockeyed for position within the family. Hannah was the pampered favourite wife of Elkanah but had borne, as yet, no children while Peninnah, his other wife, had a batch of them. Although Elkanah loved her dearly and showered her with gifts and attention, Hannah could not bear being denied something that seemed to be so freely granted to other, less cherished women. She was accustomed to getting everything she desired, and she fancied that what she most desired was a child. And Peninnah was just plain mean, constantly taunting her with her barrenness. Finally Hannah was driven to pray in the temple.

"Lord, I do so want a son of my own. Just everyone has one, even...well...just everyone! It's not fair." She pouted a little; then, trying a less familiar tactic, she rearranged her pretty face in a more devout configuration. "Only grant me this one request, Lord, and I promise to dedicate the boy to your service." She paused, imagining how admirable her selflessness must appear. Clasping her hands dramatically, she allowed tears to pool in her raised eyes.

There! That should do it, she thought.

It did.

Her joy at the subsequent birth of her son, Samuel, was dampened a bit by the knowledge that she must relinquish the boy to a life of service in the temple, but she consoled herself with the assurance that his priestly dedication would reflect well on his mother. In order to ensure that her sacrifice could not be overlooked, she composed a flattering prayer of thanksgiving, praising God.

"One small thing, though..." she added. "Besides making the barren fruitful, you might think about devising some kind of levelling handicap for women who have borne more than their share of children, especially if they are altogether too smug about it. Some sort of wasting disease would do nicely," she suggested. It seems she still nursed a grudge against Peninnah.

Samuel grew up devoutly enough in the temple, but when God actually began sharing his most secret plans with the young man in the dark hours of the night, the people of Israel realized that he was not just another pretty altar boy. He was a genuine prophet of The Lord—definitely more than qualification enough to warrant making him judge over Israel for the remainder of his life.

Barely had he adjusted to the responsibility of guiding a nation when the children of Israel went out to battle the Philistines. Unfortunately, the Israelites took quite a trouncing. The ark of The Lord with its precious contents was captured by the enemy and taken to the temple of the Philistine god Dagon, where it no doubt suffered the humiliation of being placed below the salt at all significant feasts. This insult did not go unnoticed by the God of Israel, who expressed his displeasure by afflicting the offending Philistine men with—severe haemorrhoids.

No sooner did this uncomfortable situation become public knowledge than a general meeting of Philistine leaders was called.

"Everyone, be seated," began the chairman. This was standard practice.

"Uh, I think I'd rather stand," demurred an elder. A general buzz of agreement suggested a consensus in favour of standing.

"Well...perhaps this once. Since the battle, we've been experiencing an awkward...um...inconvenience. It's probably purely coincidental, but it has been suggested that we might consider returning that captured ark to the Israelites. What do you think?"

There was an enthusiastic chorus of agreement from the crowd.

"Sure!"

"By all means."

"It's only neighbourly..."

"The sooner the better!"

The chief priest stepped forward with as much dignity as was possible under the circumstances. "It might be expedient to include a small gift," he suggested, "...perhaps with a suitably worded note of apology."

"But what shall we send?" they asked. "You must have something in mind..."

"As a matter of fact, I think I know just the thing," the priest assured them. "Mice. Golden mice are always a nice gift."

"Golden mice? Are you sure? And where are we going to get golden mice on such short notice?"

Obviously, this was not the first time they had been afflicted by God—the last occasion must have been a plague of rodents, because the priests happened to have a surfeit of golden mice in stock. Generously, they packed into a cart the ark itself and a gift casket containing a number of golden mice equal to the number of Philistine cities suffering the painful haemorrhoid outbreak.

The Philistine women, it must be admitted, found it quite entertaining to see their men afflicted by such an undignified curse, and showed very little sympathy.

"If the God of Israel is in the habit of visiting all manner of plagues on those who offend him," they warned, "He may well have trouble sorting out which discomfort went to whom. And golden mice, while always a welcome gift, might not be sufficiently pertinent to remind Him of the specific affliction you want removed. It might be helpful to jog His memory by including something a bit more evocative...might we suggest an appropriate number of solid gold haemorrhoids, for example?" The tears rolled down their cheeks from the effort of hiding their amusement.

To their extreme delight, the men, desperate, promptly had artisans whip up a set of five, as realistically fashioned as possible, and included them with the mice in their gift in order to indicate to The Lord very clearly which particular problem they wished him to address. The men's discomfort did, indeed, disappear following the return of the ark to the Israelites, but not before the women had ample opportunity to place a few spirited bets regarding which of their mates had posed for the goldsmiths.

Samuel took advantage of this opportunity to warn the Israelites, who were slipping comfortably back into the habit of disobedience, that they could be next on The Lord's list for the distribution of afflictions, so they straggled back to the path of righteousness and, as a reward, were promptly enabled to subdue the Philistines. He continued to guide the people faithfully, but the two sons he appointed to succeed him turned out to be something of an embarrassment, viewing the judicial post as a high return business opportunity and tailoring their decisions to the requirements of the highest bidders. Determined to avoid having their destiny guided by this unscrupulous pair, the people demanded instead that he choose a king to rule over them henceforth.

Irritably glancing around for a likely prospect, Samuel's eye fell on Saul, who had stopped in town for a short break while tracking down some stray asses. It was certainly Saul's lucky day, because Samuel's eyesight was failing, and the young man's great height easily made him stand out from the crowd. He had hoped to catch a glance at the famous prophet so he was pleasantly surprised when he found himself invited to Samuel's house for dinner. The puzzled guest found himself seated in the place of honour, fed liberally—as befitted his great height—and invited to stay the night.

As Samuel bade him goodbye the next morning, he mentioned, as casually as possible, "By the way, you've been chosen to be king of the Israelites...and don't worry about the asses...they'll be home when you get there." He anointed the startled lad with a vial of oil which he had kept handy for the purpose and assured him that it was only a matter of time before the Spirit of The Lord would descend on him, bringing with it the handy gift of prophesy.

When Samuel gathered all the tribes of Israel together in order to introduce their new king, Saul was found hiding among the luggage, wondering if he was up to this challenge when he wasn't even very proficient at locating missing livestock. At first the people, too, had doubts about Saul's ability to lead them.

"But," Samuel pointed out, testily, "can't you see that he's really *tall?*"

This somehow satisfied the Israelites—who should have noticed it on their own. But it comes as no surprise that the foes of Israel, hearing that an inexperienced ass-herder had been appointed to lead the Israelites, decided this might be a good time to stir up some trouble. However, in leading a series of successful battles Saul demonstrated to the nation one of the many advantages of having a really tall king.

During a grudge match against the Amalekites, who had ambushed the Israelites when they came out of Egypt so many years ago, The Lord—who was clearly in a bad mood that day—ordered that the Amalekites and all that they owned be utterly destroyed. Unfortunately, Saul was caught distributing the best bits amongst the Israelite leaders in clear defiance of the total destruction order and God started right away searching for a replacement king.

When Samuel, at The Lord's suggestion, traveled to Bethlehem to interview the sons of Jesse for the position of successor to the king, he was inclined to choose the oldest, because he, too, was quite tall. God, however, having noticed that Samuel's penchant for choosing a king based on superior height had not been remarkably successful, insisted that he pass up several perfectly serviceable taller lads to choose the youngest, David—a handsome shepherd of average height, with a notable talent for music. David was anointed as God's chosen, and then was left with his harp and his sheep until the time should be right for him to take his place as the king's understudy.

In the course of time, his reputation as a musician came to the attention of Saul who, suspecting that The Lord had turned against him, was suffering black bouts of depression. Thinking that a little musical diversion might lift his spirits, Saul summoned the lad and found that David, with a few deft plinks on the harp strings, was able to chase away his blues.

When war broke out yet again, the Philistines —thinking to add variety to what was becoming something of a stale pastime—sent out their champion, Goliath, to taunt the Israelites. He demanded that they send over their best man to fight him and thus decide the outcome of the battle in an innovative and entertaining fashion, and with a minimum of collateral damage.

A call went out for volunteers: "Anyone who accepts the challenge and kills Goliath will win tempting cash prizes and marry the king's eldest daughter."

No one was eager to volunteer because Goliath's height was a hair over six cubits and a span (that was very tall, indeed) and his armour was cleverly designed to make him look even bigger. Nevertheless, being an ambitious lad, young David—who was actually just there to deliver lunch to the troops—offered to give it a try. The sight of the young man facing his huge adversary with nothing but five smooth stones and a sling was not one to inspire a great deal of confidence. Goliath himself didn't know whether to be amused or insulted, and while he was deciding, David slung his best stone, hitting the giant dead centre in the forehead and toppling him flat on his face. He was probably already dead when he hit the ground but, grabbing Goliath's mighty sword, David used it to saw off his head, settling the question to the satisfaction of his fellow Israelites and ensuring his claim to the reward.

David had made a hit amongst the soldiers. Indeed, Saul's son Jonathan got so carried away that he stripped off his sword and his bow and his sash and even his robe, and stood on the battlefield in his underwear, enthusiastically pressing these gifts on the embarrassed hero. They became the very closest of friends.

On David's return from the battlefield, Saul's sleep was disturbed long into the night by the huge victory party that was being thrown for the lad, with pretty girls dancing and singing (in that delightfully flattering way dancing girls have): "Saul hath slain his thousands and David his ten thousands." This was more than irritating—it was downright unfair, because Goliath simply hadn't been *that* big! Seriously offended at coming in second best, Saul began to plot David's removal.

He had offered the hand of his eldest daughter in marriage as part of the victory prize, but by the time he got around to honouring the promise he had already married her off to someone else.

"Never mind, my boy," he offered, "I have a second daughter Michal, quite similar, who should do well for the purpose."

David agreed that one daughter was much like another.

"Of course," demurred Saul, "there's the matter of a dowry."

"But I can't *afford* a dowry," protested David. "That's why I went to the bother of winning a bride in the first place."

"Well, that is awkward. But wait! I have it! Let the dowry be one hundred Philistine foreskins. Not a penny spent!" Saul expected that a hundred maimed and resentful Philistines would surely be able to kill one musical shepherd, effectively doing his dirty work for him.

David recognized this to be an unusual sort of wedding gift, but he liked the girl well enough, so he and his men—he had become an army commander by that time—proceeded to search out and kill as many Philistines as they could find. They thought it would be easier to collect their foreskins that way...it being unlikely that they would give them up willingly. He brought back about two hundred prime foreskins (in case some were lost or stolen along the way), never imagining that Saul might see this as unnecessarily ostentatious.

Despite knowing that she had been rather an afterthought as a battle bonus, Michal was dazzled by David's stellar rise to fame and was determined to make the best of the marriage. Perceiving that her father grew every day more erratic and sensing that the warmth of his relationship with her husband had cooled—the obvious risk inherent in the foreskin wedding gift scheme had alerted her that something might be amiss—she urged her brother Jonathan to warn David of any new life-threatening plot Saul might be contemplating. However, David, flattered at having been accepted into the royal family, was remarkably slow to recognize the dramatically unfavourable change in his father-in-law's attitude toward him.

"You look a bit flushed," she noted, as David sat down to dinner one evening. "Was there some excitement at the palace today?"

"No," mumbled David, between bites. "Just a typical musical interlude. I played. I sang."

"You're home early. Are you sure nothing unusual happened?"

"Well, your father tried to nail me to the wall with his javelin..."

"My god! Are you all right?" She jumped up and ran to his side.

"Oh, sure. I just dodged the thrust and ducked out of the room."

"...and you weren't going to *tell* me?"

"Don't make such a fuss." He brushed her aside. "I knew you'd make a fuss. It's not the first time—he was simply kidding around."

Sensing that David might not survive the night unless someone took this situation more seriously, Michal convinced him to humour her by escaping out the bedroom window and fleeing, while she bravely offered to face her father's wrath and cover his retreat. As she had anticipated, Saul's servants arrived at the front door to fetch him at the very moment that David was scrambling down the trellis in back. Showing them what appeared to be David bundled up in the bed, she claimed he was much too ill to attend, thus buying her husband a few precious hours of escape time. By the time they returned with orders to carry him, sick as he was, to Saul, they found only a large and rather heavy statue which Michal had wrestled onto the bed, stuffing a goat's hair pillow under its head and tucking a blanket around it as realistically as time had allowed. Predictably, Saul was enraged at his daughter's ruse, and she narrowly escaped who knows what severe punishment by convincing him that David had threatened her life, forcing her to comply with his nefarious scheme.

David took advantage of this opportunity to visit awhile with Samuel, spending the interlude pleasantly enough cooking up prophesies together, but when Saul's messengers were continually spotted in the neighbourhood searching for him, he began to wonder whether Michal's concerns regarding her father's murderous intentions might have had some merit after all. He snuck back and secretly contacted Jonathan.

"What's eating your father, anyway?" David demanded. "What did *I* do?"

His friend, who was the teeniest bit self-absorbed, hadn't noticed anything at all unusual in his father's demeanour, but he agreed to ascertain as discreetly as possible whether it was safe for David to return. In fact, it seemed an amusing bit of intrigue to Jonathan. He was at loose ends at the time and entertained himself by devising an unnecessarily elaborate scheme for conveying the results of his probe to David—something involving a sports outing and a servant boy fetching errant arrows and the delivery of secretly meaningful code words and other such entertaining devices.

At dinner that night, Jonathan searched for the most diplomatic way to bring up the issue.

"So...why have you been trying to kill David?" he blurted out. "What did he ever do to you?"

Grabbing the javelin which he kept by his side constantly now for just such impromptu occasions, Saul promptly attempted to skewer his disloyal son—making his position crystal clear to the most obtuse of observers. Now thoroughly alarmed, Jonathan hastened to advise David that a prompt and permanent retreat would be expedient, as no reconciliation seemed likely any time soon. (He almost forgot, in his agitation, to implement the cunning plan about the arrows and the servant and the secret code, which would have been a great shame.)

Thinking to hide in the city of Gath but fearing that his reputation might be somewhat intimidating, David attempted to make himself appear less imposing by scrabbling at the gate and drooling down his beard, like a madman. His portrayal was very convincing—perhaps too convincing, in fact. The king of Gath saw no immediate need for additional madmen, the gate remained locked, and David was forced to revise his plans and move on. He collected a sizable band of debtors and malcontents about him and fled across the countryside with Saul hot on his trail.

Once, Saul got so close that David was able to sneak up on him playfully in the night and cut the hem off his robe. It seemed like a good joke at the time, but when he saw how ridiculous the king looked the next day, trudging along in little more than his shirt tails, David regretted his humiliating little lark and approached Saul to make an attempt at reconciliation.

"Sire, you appear to have lost something," taunted David, despite his good intentions. He waved a suspiciously familiar piece of frayed fabric.

The king stared at the cloth, and said nothing.

"I knew you'd be one to appreciate a good prank. You see how easily I could have killed you if I'd wanted to—but I didn't do it."

"No," Saul admitted, "you didn't. Thanks so much for showing such noble restraint. I can't thank you enough! What can I possibly do to repay you?" A more sensitive man than David might have noticed the dangerous glitter in the king's eye.

"Well, you might stop hunting me down like a dog," suggested David.

"Of course, my boy! I should have thought of that myself. Consider it done."

By this time Saul was irritating everyone around him with his paranoid whining; he heard a threat in every footfall and saw a conspirator behind every bush. And this latest bit of tomfoolery, while harmless in itself, hadn't done much to improve matters. Despite his promise, Saul continued to pursue David just as relentlessly as ever. The king was obsessed with the idea that the younger man was a threat to his throne, if not his life—and, to be sure, he wasn't far wrong.

As they wandered across the countryside, David and his men found it necessary to think creatively about making a living. Obviously, they were too peripatetic for farming or herding to be considered an option. Approaching the lands of the wealthy Nabal as he was celebrating a successful sheep-shearing, David sent a small but intimidating delegation of his men to demand a free meal for himself and six hundred of his closest friends on the grounds that they had refrained from robbing and killing the shepherds...until now. Nabal, who was a churlish drunk at the best of times, rudely refused what to a modern ear might sound suspiciously like the initial demands of a fledgling protection racket. David was displeased with the outcome of what had seemed like a promising career path, and began considering more violent methods of feeding his gang of followers.

When Nabal's beautiful wife Abigail heard of her husband's rash words, she hastened to repair the damage before the wrath of David fell on her family. She had already begun to hear rumours that David was preparing to kill everyone in the household who pissed against a wall. Not that she felt the women were in any danger of attack, as they rarely even attempted to piss against a wall. But rape remained a distinct and unappealing probability so she was determined to defuse the situation.

Unbeknownst to Nabal, who was still partying and could be counted upon to continue to do so for some time, she quickly put together a huge picnic lunch and personally delivered it to David for his men.

"I would have come earlier," she assured him, "if I'd only known you were hungry. My husband doesn't always handle these situations with sufficient tact."

"He was a boor," commented David.

"And you're not the first to notice it. But I've heard some very impressive things about *you*. I felt certain that someone like yourself, who is doing God's work, would not want to appear unfair before The Lord by punishing my family just because I've arrived a little late with the snacks." Her smile suggested that she was sure fairness was only one of his many sterling qualities.

"Of course," he conceded, "I wouldn't want to be unnecessarily harsh. When a pretty lady goes to such trouble, it can never be too late."

"Then I'm sure you'll agree that the weapons of your men can be better utilized against your real enemies than wasted on my drunken fool of a husband," she suggested, pointedly.

Swayed by her charm, David agreed to spare them. As she had expected, she returned home to find that her absence hadn't even been noticed by her husband, who continued to carouse. And when Nabal suddenly dropped dead about a week and a half later, she certainly didn't miss *him* overmuch.

Unfortunately, Abigail hadn't thought to wear a bag over her pretty head when she had met with David so, on hearing that she was free, he immediately decided to marry her himself. (He'd quite forgotten about Michal by this time.) She was rather disappointed, as she'd been looking eagerly forward to being on her own, with her husband's fortune and no one to answer to but she was of a philosophical turn of mind, and resigned herself to the marriage. After all, David would be occupied most of the time fighting The Lord's battles, so how bad could it be? This question was soon answered when, in no time at all, he also married a girl named Ahinoam. Admitting to herself that it had never been much of a love match anyway, Abigail sighed, and prepared to make friends with Ahinoam, who was probably no more thrilled with the situation than she was.

Saul had been in the habit of asking Samuel for advice before each major battle, but eventually Samuel died, and was unavailable for consultation. The king had banished all mystics and wizards and soothsayers when he found that they occasionally said sooths he didn't like, and since God was displeased with him, the Israelite prophets were unlikely to be of much help to him either. Lost without some form of guidance, he sent his servants to make secret enquiries, and heard of a woman at Endor—a follower of the Earth Goddess—whose many abilities included a talent for communing with the dead. Being pressed for time and suspecting that she wouldn't respond eagerly to a summons to his royal environs he disguised himself and, under cover of darkness, surreptitiously visited her cottage.

"I heard you can call up the dead," he blurted out. He was not accustomed to beat around the bush. "I need to get in touch with the prophet Samuel...now!"

Of course, the disguise was of no use at all, because a woman who could contact the dead was unlikely to be tricked by a set of unfamiliar garments and a dab of hastily applied makeup. She knew a tall king when she saw one.

"Well, that would be a dangerous talent to have, wouldn't it?" she answered, cautiously. "I believe the king banished all soothsayers some time ago. You must be mistaken."

"Look," he pleaded, "I don't have time for this. I need some advice, and Samuel was always so *helpful.*"

"Sorry."

"Ok, ok. I'm King Saul...."

She tossed him a token look of surprise.

"...and I swear you won't be punished for staying in the country contrary to my orders."

She must have held a bit of a grudge over a piece of legislation which had undoubtedly impacted negatively on the volume of her business, but she generously laid her personal grievances aside and attempted to do her civic duty by being as helpful as possible. When she had successfully contacted Samuel (Saul recognized him from her description of his clothes; clearly *Samuel* was too dignified to appear in disguise), she conveyed the king's urgent request for advice on the war.

"He's a little irritated at being disturbed," she told Saul. "He's muttering something unflattering about your decision-making abilities."

Saul flushed. "I know I should be able to get along without him, but I'm afraid..."

"He says you have good reason to be afraid," she interrupted. "The Lord most certainly does intend to take the kingdom away from you, and..." she added, "he's planning to give it to David."

The king leaped to his feet, choking with rage.

"And, by the way," she added, "you and three of your sons will fall to the Philistines in the coming battle. Is that what you wanted to know?"

Saul fainted dead away. He later insisted that it was because he hadn't eaten since early the day before, but it was hard to mistake the look of abject terror on his royal countenance.

The woman compassionately threw a pitcher of water on the distraught king (she enjoyed this part more than, perhaps, she should have), fed him a nourishing meal, lifted his spirits a trifle with some of her more entertaining predictions and when his garments were sufficiently dry, sent him sneaking away into the night.

In the course of time, David did become ruler of the kingdom and Saul and all three of the sons she had mentioned did, indeed, die in the battle.

When Saul was mortally wounded, he attempted suicide rather than risk mutilation at the hands of the enemy. Unfortunately, this was only partially effective, as they found his corpse after the fact, cut off his head and rather vindictively nailed his body to a wall. Then, to add insult to injury, they put together a traveling head-on-a stick show, fastening it finally in their temple, for the ongoing amusement of their own god, Dagon. Probably this was exactly the kind of thing Saul had wanted to avoid.

Despite the fact that the test of a true prophet rested on whether the prophesies came to pass, we're somehow not surprised that the woman of Endor was never given the honour of that coveted title. In fact, she was never even paid for the dinner. Nevertheless, all things weighed in the balance, she considered herself lucky that Saul kept his promise and did not put her to death for her troubles. (Perhaps he would have, after all, if he'd lived long enough.)

Returning to Hebron after Saul's death, David was duly anointed as king of Judah and insisted on the return of his first wife Michal as a condition of employment. When David *had* bolted out of their bedroom window, so long ago, Saul had promptly married Michal off to a worthy man named Phaltiel. Nevertheless, David had delivered those two hundred Philistine foreskins as a wedding gift and he was entitled to reclaim his reward, so Phaltiel was simply out of luck. If he had been able to gather two hundred Philistine foreskins of his own, his claim might have been considered, but he just wasn't in that line of work.

Michal was summarily plucked from her home with Phaltiel and shipped along to David and, to tell the truth, she didn't put up a lot of resistance because she had been remembering him fondly ever since his dramatic escape so long ago.

After some of the loose ends had been tied up by a few murders—of which David assured everyone he was entirely blameless—and a handful of very brutal executions, David had the support he needed in order to become king over all Israel—and he was barely thirty years old. The ark of God was carried to rest in Zion, which he chose to call the City of David (naturally) and he himself most enthusiastically danced in the ceremonial parade. Seeing him from her window after all this time, leaping and prancing in the streets in nothing but a linen loincloth, Michal thought he looked like a fool, and began to wonder why she'd carried a torch for him for all these years.

She may also have been a little miffed at finding six new wives already ensconced in her new home, for David hadn't been satisfied to stop at marrying Abigail and Ahinoam; furthermore, on his arrival, he lost no time picking through all the girls of Jerusalem and adding the choicest of the lot to the crowd as well.

When David returned home after the festivities, Michal didn't hesitate to speak her mind. "Well," she snapped, "you made a fine spectacle of yourself today, sporting about before the servant girls in nothing but your underwear!"

"That's a fine greeting," he complained. "I was dancing in honour of The Lord. It was my way of celebrating, and I'll have you know that I won't hesitate to demean myself even further, if I so choose.

"And," he shouted, "all the servant girls *loved* my dance...they told me so. *They* know how to appreciate a man!"

This had definitely not been an auspicious beginning to their new life together. In fact, Michal was so disgusted that she was content to remain childless for the remainder of her life rather than encourage David to prance back into her bed.

After David was finished fighting the Philistines and had expended a significant amount of time and energy battling the Syrians, he thought he might enjoy spending more time at home, so he allowed his commander Joab to take over for a while. This left him with a lot of time on his hands and, in his search for diversion, he developed the unattractive habit of creeping up onto the roof of his palace in the middle of the night to see what his subjects were up to. On one such night, he hit the jackpot. The lovely Bathsheba, wife of Uriah the Hittite, forgetting that the height of the darkened palace would give any roof-top watcher a clear view, was cooling off after a sweltering day by bathing before her open window. It opened only onto an inner courtyard so, except for royal peepers, her privacy would have been complete.

Imagine her surprise when she received a nocturnal invitation to join the king at the palace, alone—framed in words which allowed no option of refusal. Having previewed the package, David was determined to sample the goods. Knowing the king's reputation, she could have no doubt at all of his intentions. It was unthinkable to refuse his command, but Bathsheba was a decent woman, and loved her husband deeply. He was a plain man—a soldier—but a man of honour. To her chagrin, he was at this time an absent man of honour, as he was off fighting David's enemies. (This detail had not escaped the king's notice.) So she summoned all her courage, hoping to defuse David's ardour by a reasoned appeal to his sense of decency.

She soon found that his particular courtship style left little scope for subtlety and even less opportunity for conversation. The thought that any woman might prefer to avoid his royal attentions never entered his head, and if it had, it's not at all certain that he would have cared. Ignoring her desperate protests, he demonstrated quite graphically what he wanted of her and told her to consider her dance card filled for an indefinite period of time. Any more vigorous show of resistance was sure to be dangerous for both herself and her husband, so Bathsheba submitted, and hid her shame and outrage in her heart.

Before long, she had become pregnant and David found himself faced with a quandary. He'd been much too busy amusing himself with Bathsheba to be the least bit discreet—he had spent a *lot* of time with her. And he wasn't tired of her yet. But it was unlikely that her husband would be obliging enough to overlook the fact that he had been out of town at the time of conception. He was bound to notice. It was going to look very bad.

Hurriedly David summoned Uriah from the battlefield.

"Uriah. I, uh, need an update on the progress of the battle," he confided, "and I know I can rely on you to give me an honest report."

Uriah was confused. He had only seen the king a few times before, at a distance, and had never spoken to him in person at all. "Well...." he stammered, "I wasn't prepared...I mean, it's going as well as..."

"Good...good." David interrupted, impatiently. "And the men...are they in good spirits?"

"I think...when I left them, they..."

"Fine. Good man! I know you have their loyalty. You've been doing a wonderful job out there! But you must be exhausted. I want you to take the rest of the night off." He threw his arm around the startled soldier. "Go home to bed. With your wife. You can return to your post in the morning."

David hoped that in this way, Uriah would be able to assume that the child was his own. It was the best plan he could think of on the spur of the moment. It wasn't a *great* plan, but he'd considered and rejected several even more ridiculous ones before selecting it. He didn't feel that this was something he could discuss with his advisors, so he was on his own, and it wasn't easy.

Unfortunately, Uriah felt it would be contemptible to dally while his troops slept on the hard ground, preparing for battle. After an abortive attempt to get Uriah drunk enough to forget his duty and tumble into bed with his wife—even in a drunken stupor, this frustrating man refused to abandon his ethics—David realized he was manoeuvring in unfamiliar territory, and he decided that the situation called for more forthright measures.

He promptly wrote to Joab, who was directing the siege of the city of Rabbah.

"I was most impressed with the succinct report Uriah was able to give me on the progress of the battle. I think he's wasted in his present command. I want you to send him to the front lines where the risk from spears and flying missiles is always high...or failing that, a big rock might fall on his head—it's been known to happen...His dedication to duty will be an inspiration to the troops there."

Joab knew of Bathsheba, and understood exactly what was required of him.

As expected, David soon received the welcome news that Uriah had been killed in the battle. The coincidence of her husband's death was not lost on Bathsheba, as she had learned at first hand David's propensity for sweeping aside any impediment to his convenience. She was distraught at having been unwittingly the cause of her husband's demise and grief weighed on her spirit, but she had her unborn child to think of. She was hurriedly added to the king's stable of wives, and subsequently gave birth to a son. Even David couldn't fail to notice that she was no longer a fun date.

David was hoping to forget the whole sordid mess, but Nathan the prophet was tipped off by God, who must have felt that David had crossed some fine ethical line in this matter.

Nathan presented a little riddle to the king:

"What if a very rich man were entertaining a guest and, rather than butcher one of his own many sheep for the feast, he chose instead to steal and slaughter the single lamb belonging to his poor neighbour. What should be his punishment?"

David was appalled. "The selfish cad should be killed!" he declared.

When Nathan revealed that the selfish cad in the story represented the king himself, David wished he had listened to the details of the story more carefully and been a bit more prudent in his recommendation.

But The Lord had his own ideas regarding an appropriate punishment. After throwing a scare into David by threatening to take away all his wives and distribute them among his neighbours (there were probably enough to supply the men in the adjacent communities as well), God unaccountably settled for killing Bathsheba's innocent newborn son. While the infant was ill, David fasted and wept and carried on in a most dramatic manner but as soon as it was dead, he cleaned himself up, packed down a hearty meal and sought out Bathsheba, thinking that a quick roll in the sheets might console her in her grief. Nine months later, Solomon was born, effectively replacing David's loss. So his selfish act of lust had resulted in the death of a good man and a helpless baby, had caused Bathsheba incalculable anguish, and had made David miss a couple of meals.

King David's penchant for gathering wives about him was bound to result in tragedy, sooner or later. As the multitude of his offspring grew to adolescence with hormones raging, anyone less self-involved than the king would have recognized a disaster, just waiting to happen.

Sure enough, Amnon, one of David's many sons, developed an unwelcome carnal passion for his half-sister Tamar.

Unaccustomed as he was to having his desires denied, Amnon didn't consider consulting *her* opinion on the matter and simply took what he wanted by force.

When Absalom, one of her many other brothers (they were very close...but in a *good* way), noticed that King David didn't seem inclined to do much of anything about this, he avenged his sister's honour in his own way. Waiting until Amnon was enjoying a drunken carouse, sodden and vulnerable, he had him murdered.

Fearing the king's wrath at being deprived of a son, Absalom fled. He was eventually reconciled with his father, but he never completely forgave David for his lack of any real concern for poor Tamar. The young man began to gather chariots and a bodyguard about him and hang around the palace, drumming up support among the people who approached the king for justice.

"I wish I could help you," he commiserated. "Seems like it's always either justice denied or justice delayed. But I have no power, you know."

And: "It's a shame. I'm sure I could arrange things so much better if I were in charge..." he would mutter, in a deceptively off-handed manner, as he turned away.

After forty years of campaigning—shaking all the right hands and kissing not only the babies but their fathers as well, where necessary—he felt he was popular enough to make his move. Politics was in its infancy then, so these things took a lot longer than they do today.

He wheedled David's permission to go to Hebron, where he promptly established himself as a rival to his father. There followed the requisite period of manoeuvring and back-biting, complete with the traditional spies in high places, false advice and assassination plots, terminating in a great final battle between the forces of father and son.

As Absalom dashed confidently off to battle on the back of his favourite war mule, fate, which was in a playful mood that day, directed him beneath the low boughs of an old oak tree. Somehow he got his head caught in the branches and stopped short, while the mule galloped disloyally along, leaving him dangling there ignominiously, like a large ripe fruit. This was too good an opportunity to miss, so after everyone had a good laugh at his expense, David's commander Joab pierced the helpless Absalom in the heart with three darts, leaving him quite dead.

When David heard of this, he wept with grief. Fortunately, he had other rebellious enemies ready to distract his attention.

The most dangerous of these was Sheba, who led Israel against David and the men of Judah. When Joab and his men cornered him at the city of Abel, Sheba strode boldly into the city, as was usual in such cases, declaring to the townspeople, "I'm here now, and you just have to fight to protect me." One of the most respected of the town councillors—a very wise woman—responded calmly, "You know...I'm not sure that we do!" And they prudently restrained Sheba in a suitably secure facility, pending further developments.

When David's army began to batter at the walls, this brave old woman agreed to go out to speak with

Joab on behalf of her neighbours, hoping to avoid the destruction of the city, with all the rape and slaughter that was customary at such times.

"You, sir, appear to be a clear-thinking man," began this astute diplomat. "Have you considered the waste of valuable resources that will result from the unnecessary destruction of yet another town? I'm sure we can work out a more practical arrangement. Which issues do you consider non-negotiable?"

"We want Sheba," grunted Joab, tersely.

"There...you see! I like a man who comes straight to the point. That doesn't sound unreasonable...I'm sure we can work something out."

Before their meeting concluded, she was able to negotiate a most satisfactory trade. Having solemnly weighed the number of lives at risk, she agreed that the townspeople would deliver the head of Sheba, suitable for mounting as a trophy. In return, Joab would immediately take his soldiers and leave. The head was duly severed and thrown out over the walls to Joab...and the soldiers obligingly moved on. All in all, it was a good deal—although Sheba probably wouldn't have thought so.

No sooner had all this been cleared up than the Philistines, hoping to take advantage of the distraction, started yet another war with Israel. David joined the battle in person this time, but he was no longer the man he had been. When a giant son of his old foe Goliath challenged him, the king fainted dead away and one of his commanders had to step in to slay the brute. David's men begged him to stay behind the lines; he was becoming an embarrassment in the field. Even so, they were obliged to fight and kill three more of

Goliath's sons (or one might have been his brother...the record is unclear)—all gigantic and all eager to make a name for themselves—before the Philistines accepted the fact that the fearsome shepherd-king would no longer come out to fight.

Rather shaken by his unfortunate fainting spell, David agreed to keep well back from the field of battle, and spent his time comfortably holed up in a cave, composing a catchy tune praising God and thanking him for all his help over the years. Naturally, he couldn't resist taking this opportunity to point out to The Lord how richly he had deserved every last favour, due to his outstanding righteousness, remarkably clean living and unfailing obedience.

Perhaps in a sportive attempt to test the true level of David's selflessness, or maybe just on a whim, God presented the old king with three options. "You can choose seven years of famine for the land, three days of pestilence for the people, or three months fleeing from your enemies," said The Lord. "Pick one."

The king had been looking forward eagerly to a little rest and relaxation at home, so he wearily left the choice in The Lord's hands...as long as the enemy pursuit option was taken off the table. Complacently, God chose to send the pestilence, sweeping seventy thousand Israelites from the land in no time.

Feeling an unpleasant twinge of guilt for relaxing comfortably with his family while his subjects perished, David asked The Lord for a do-over. "Is it too late to change my mind? I'd like to switch to an option that would fall on myself and my family alone and spare the rest of my people." He made this noble gesture without consulting any family members, of course, but then his family was a large one, and not easy to round up for a consensus.

The plague was duly lifted, but God was already losing interest in the game so he generously agreed to take an offering of fifty silver shekels worth of oxen, and call it even.

Chapter 9

More Kings and a Couple of Queens

As King David shuffled toward the precipice of death, his attention was fully occupied with the few small comforts that were left to him, and he didn't much care who took the reins of the kingdom when he was gone. Seeing a potential career opportunity opening up, his son Adonijah began building a base of power. But he didn't reckon on Bathsheba. At the time of her son Solomon's birth, she had elicited a vow from David that the child would succeed him as king. And Bathsheba had sacrificed far too much to the king to watch this go wrong.

"You made me a solemn vow, David," she reminded him. "Do you really think your life has been so spotless that you can risk offending The Lord by ignoring a solemn vow? Surely you don't want me to remind you of some of the highlights."

David stared at her in amazement. "Are you threatening me?"

"Just don't try me further. I know what I know."

When David made it clear that this younger son was to succeed him, Adonijah realized he was treading in political quicksand and, swallowing his disappointment, he complied immediately. That wasn't quick enough to suit Solomon, who lost no time finding pretexts, however flimsy, to have his brother killed—along with any other old enemies his father had promised to spare. His conscience might have troubled him more regarding these executions if David himself had not slyly suggested with his dying breath that any promises of leniency he'd found it expedient to make over the years need not be taken too seriously by his successor.

One night—fortunately, it was early in Solomon's reign—The Lord appeared to him in a dream and offered to grant him a wish. Dabbling in the shallow end of the waters of diplomacy, the young man tactfully asked only that he be granted the gift of a wise and understanding heart with which to judge his people—and God knew he needed one. His gamble paid off. The Lord, impressed that he had asked nothing for himself, not only granted Solomon the wisdom he had requested, he also generously threw in the unasked riches and honours and, as an additional bonus, a long life—but only if he behaved himself to God's complete satisfaction.

Solomon tried out his new wisdom on two women who appeared before him for a decision—one which would determine not only the course of their lives but that of an innocent child as well.

Both unmarried, they lived together and each had recently given birth. Tragically, in her sleep one night, one of the women had rolled over and smothered her infant. Awaking to find the child dead, and maddened with grief, she took the live baby from the arms of her still sleeping companion and replaced it with the small corpse. A desperate quarrel ensued when morning came and the switch was detected, with each woman insisting that the live infant was her own. How was the king to judge between the two, with a child's fate at stake?

As the women fought over the infant, the king's patience wore thin. "Stop that wrangling immediately!" snapped the king. "The child will be sliced in two pieces, and an equal portion will be given to each. There! Guards!"

The child's mother, heartbroken, immediately offered to give up the baby, begging only that its life be spared. The other was perfectly willing to accept the division of the small body, so long as she got her share.

Now, this seemed just *wrong*.

Rethinking his decision, Solomon ordered that the child be presented, intact, to the woman who had selflessly pleaded for its welfare.

It was assumed that Solomon had cleverly designed the threat to flush out the identity of the natural mother, knowing that her maternal instinct would compel her to protect her child from harm. That, of course, is possible—especially in view of the wise and understanding heart with which The Lord had so recently endowed him. It's equally possible that Solomon simply got fed up with the quarrelling and ordered the division of the child as the first convenient solution that suggested itself to him. Whatever the truth may be, he made the right decision in the end and gave the child into the care of a devoted mother rather than that of a raving lunatic...for which, I suppose, he must be commended.

It was on this and other equally challenging decisions that Solomon's reputation for wisdom was built. When the Queen of Sheba, a country rich in precious stones and spices, arrived at Solomon's court with lavish gifts, she was determined to test his sagacity. Solomon—astutely recognizing that she was a female, and a wealthy one at that—wasted no time before offering to add her to his stable of mates. (This seems to have been an obsessive family habit, inherited from his father.)

"I find you tolerably attractive," he assured her, suavely "and there's always room for one more."

"As flattering as your offer is," responded the Queen, graciously, "I, myself, am much more drawn to your reputed wisdom than to its mere physical vessel. I'm afraid that I must decline." Obviously, she did not consider physical attraction to be *his* strongest suit either.

This issue being so gracefully disposed of, they were able to move on to other business. While all other rulers had been content to make the decision to pay tribute to Israel based on their ability to resist, she had come to test Solomon's depth of understanding. Only after quizzing him in person and at length was she satisfied that he had the ability to govern wisely the lands under his protection and only then did she give the order that the tribute he demanded should be relinquished. Her lands were rich and distant, giving them a certain measure of security from the threat of actual attack, so her decision stands as concrete testimony that his legendary wisdom may well have been something more than just propaganda cooked up by some ancient public relations department.

As king, Solomon was entitled to a certain level of self-indulgence, but when his household tally reached seven hundred wives and three hundred concubines, he began to look a little greedy even to God, who had tolerantly overlooked the escalating degree of such acquisitive behaviour in the Israelite kings up to that time. His passion for owning the most desirable of everything eventually led him to collect his wives from among the most beautiful women in all the lands at his disposal, rather than limiting himself to Israelites alone. Common sense and a basic knowledge of arithmetic would suggest to even the most casual of observers that the amount of attention each woman received from the king must have been minimal, at best, and as he aged and his capacity to distract them diminished, they had even more than the usual amount of excess time on their hands. Much of this time they devoted to the worship of their various foreign gods and goddesses. At first, Solomon merely tolerated their activities as harmless amusements which kept them from nagging him about his flagging attentions. Eventually, however, he became intrigued with their exotic deities and agreed to join in some of their kinkier rituals. Needless to say, God was not even the least little bit amused. He resolved to withdraw his support from the house of Solomon the very next time that the monarchy of Israel was in question—retaining, of course, the option of changing his mind at a moment's notice.

When Solomon finally died after having reined for forty years, it became apparent that his wisdom had turned out to be more of the flashy courtroom variety than the every-day, helpfully understanding-heart sort. But the people's pleas for relief from the old king's oppressive rule and constant demands for tribute were met unsympathetically by his son Rehoboam.

"Keep whining and you'll see how bad things can get!" he snarled. And his threat to torture them with scorpions, while creative in its way, was not likely to create any noticeable degree of good will.

"I have more power in my little finger", he bragged, "than my father had in his whole penis,"...which may have been true, towards the end, but was hardly to the point. The disgusted Israelites discarded Rehoboam and, just to irritate him, chose Jeroboam, the son of one of Solomon's servants, to rule in his place; only the tribe of Judah and the city of Jerusalem remained loyal to Rehoboam.

Sadly, Jeroboam and his successors proved to be an unfortunate choice to rule over the people of Israel, filling the subsequent years with all the usual wars and treachery and idolatry...while Solomon's successors in Judah were often not one bit better.

When Ahab became king of Israel, and chose to marry a Zidonian woman named Jezebel, God had reason to be especially displeased. Though feigning to worship the god Baal, which was bad enough, her true allegiance was to the more ancient and democratic Earth Goddess...and Ahab was devoted to Jezebel. He even went so far as to build her a sizable grove, suitable for stocking with whatever gods or goddesses suited her fancy.

"And shall I worship at your altar, my love?" he asked.

"Ah, no," she responded. "My deity is my own. You must build your own, to honour whatever gods suit you!"

"But I don't know how to begin."

"Then I shall help you, my dear."

In leading him to seek out a personal divinity and style of worship, she found herself playfully teaching the Israelites dietary and sexual rituals differing in some radical ways from those which the God of Israel had specifically recommended. Her innovations were welcomed with most gratifying enthusiasm.

These things have a way of escalating beyond all reason. As a part of her rather over-enthusiastic program of reform, Jezebel decided that there were altogether too many prophets of The Lord wandering about the countryside, and ordered that they all be destroyed. (It must be admitted that there were an awful lot of them at the time.) But God ensured the survival of the prophet Elijah by urging this as a prudent time for him to leave on a camping trip. Why, The Lord occasionally even took time out of his busy day to send ravens winging their way to Elijah with snacks when provisions were scarce. Elijah was clearly a favourite.

Elijah came to public attention during a terrible drought, which the prophets of Baal were attempting to end. He was determined to show that The Lord was the one true god, so he challenged all four hundred and fifty of the prophets of Baal as well as about four hundred scruffy individuals passing as grove prophets to a contest. (There appears to have been a bumper crop of prophets on all sides that year.)

Elijah chose a bullock and Baal's prophets chose a bullock. Each animal was cut in bits and laid on a pile of wood with no fire under, to see which god would first miraculously set his particular offering alight. Predictably, the bullock dedicated to Baal failed to burn, despite the fact that his prophets were dancing and cavorting spiritedly on the altar in their efforts to attract their god's attention.

"Yell louder!" taunted Elijah. "If Baal is talking, he may not be able to hear you over the sound of his own voice. Or perhaps he's gone on a short vacation...or maybe he merely nodded off for a moment. But don't rush him...we can wait."

When it became clear that Baal was not going to come through for them, Elijah stepped up to The Lord's altar, determined to put on a good show.

"Douse the bullock with water," he insisted. "No, I'm not kidding...the firewood too. Go ahead...barrels and barrels of water. And again...throw it on there! And one more time!" By this time, the altar was sodden, Elijah stood ankle deep in a pool of water, and the audience was shuffling in every direction in an effort to avoid soaking their sandals in stray rivulets.

The Lord, who had been alertly awaiting his cue, caused not only the firewood and the bullock but the very stones and dust and the water that soaked them to burst impressively into flames. So the true God prevailed and the people were won over—at least for a time. Elijah took advantage of this opportunity to have them slaughter all four hundred and fifty of the rival prophets of Baal. (He didn't bother about the grove priests...they hadn't put on much of a show, and weren't serious contenders.) The subsequent picnic celebration was rained out by an ambitious little cloud summoned out of the sea by Elijah, but the drought was finally ended so nobody minded. They simply moved the eats indoors, and went right on partying.

When she heard about the contest and the massacre and the festivities—to which she, understandably, had not been invited—Jezebel flew into a rage and threatened to kill Elijah before another day passed. The mass murder of prophets just didn't seem nearly so funny when it was somebody else's idea. So Elijah prudently ran off into the wilderness to hide under a juniper tree for a while.

This time was not entirely wasted. After his fear abated and he had done some hiking in the wilderness, God led him to the young farmer Elisha who was to start training in prophesies immediately, as his apprentice.

Life was not all battles for the kings of Israel, but they had a bad habit of getting into trouble with The Lord whenever they had time on their hands. During one of these times of hiatus, Ahab got an unaccountable whim to possess the vineyard belonging to a man named Naboth. It was situated very near the palace grounds...perhaps he wanted to pull up the vines and open up a broad stretch for lawn bowling.

When Naboth proved unwilling to sell him the land, Ahab felt sure that life held no further pleasure for him, so he retired to his bed with a sick headache, turned his face to the wall, and refused to eat a bite. His wife Jezebel found this petulance most unattractive in a grown man, but he had always been an indulgent husband so she determined to solve this problem in the most expeditious way possible, before his childish conduct seriously damaged their relationship.

"Stop being such a big baby!" she suggested...as sympathetically as possible. "You'll get your land."

Using Ahab's considerable influence, she had Naboth promoted to a lofty position, then arranged to have him denounced as a blasphemer against God and the king. That would have been enough...he would have had to forfeit the vineyard in question, and since God had no pressing use for it, it would have come to Ahab by default. But she hadn't figured on the enthusiasm of the Israelite crowd who took this opportunity to have a bit of sport, and proceeded to stone poor Naboth to death.

Jezebel shrugged her pretty shoulders and casually informed Ahab that Naboth had been killed, and the land was now his. Drying his tears of frustration and sniffing pathetically a couple of times, he scurried off to seize the land in question before some pesky relative of the dead man could claim it. Unfortunately, God had taken offence at some of the more unscrupulous aspects of this land-grab, and he sent Elijah to chide Ahab for the scurvy plot.

"A blatant injustice has been perpetrated on an innocent man," declared the prophet. "Furthermore, the scheme lacked subtlety and discretion and thus was unworthy of a servant of The Lord. In consequence, all those who piss against a wall will turn against you...just as soon as they notice." He specified no particular wall and, since wall-pissing was clearly a widespread habit at that time, we must assume that he meant all men in a general way—and perhaps any women who indulged in wall-pissing as well, although these probably amounted to a relatively insignificant percentage of the total.

"And the dogs that licked Naboth's blood would do well to hang around for a while," he added, "because they'll get their chance to snack on yours as well."

Ahab protested in vain that he had known nothing of Jezebel's ill-conceived plot. Elijah was unshaken in his resolve to provide an additional treat for the dogs, and he was even more delighted to add Jezebel to the menu, vowing that she in her turn would be devoured, near by the town wall.

He had not forgotten her part in the execution of so many of his fellow prophets.

❖

Ahab was succeeded by one son after another, and the royal house of Israel showed no signs of renouncing their pagan habits. Eventually God decided that a change was long past due, so he encouraged a particularly ambitious army captain named Jehu to try for the position of king. As the post was already filled by Ahab's son Joram, Jehu would have to fight for his throne. But it represented a huge promotion and the perks were attractive, so Jehu eagerly agreed to give it a try. With The Lord meddling in the affair, it wasn't much of a contest. Joram was killed in battle and Israel had a fresh king.

While he was in the neighbourhood, Jehu dropped by the royal house, thinking to amuse himself by watching Jezebel grovel. His victory had made Jehu much too big for his britches, and he shouted an arrogant challenge up at her window: "Bring forth the whore Jezebel, so that she can crawl at my feet!"

As Jezebel had no grovelling in mind, his words were met with a resounding silence. She had been mourning the death of her son, but having been warned of Jehu's arrival, Jezebel was determined not to give him the satisfaction of viewing her grief. She had dressed herself with care, hiding her pallor with makeup, and she appeared majestically at the window wearing the stateliest of her royal headdresses. Jehu, watching below, felt like a country bumpkin in the presence of such tragic dignity, and this didn't improve his temper at all.

Noticing two or three of her house eunuchs cowering behind her, Jehu shouted, bravely, "Who's on my side? Throw the witch down!"

Hoping to gain the goodwill of the king *du jour,* these paragons of loyalty promptly complied, obligingly pitching Jezebel down onto the pavement below.

Her blood spattered the wall and the horses, and made a terrible mess in the courtyard. After entertaining himself for a bit, treading on her lifeless body, Jehu rode off to clean himself up and celebrate with his colleagues in arms—in some even less regal manner, no doubt. By the time they came back to bury her, the ever-famished dogs had devoured all but a few oddly assorted bits: her skull, her feet, and the palms of her hands. Elijah was, no doubt, most gratified...and perhaps there was some symbolic meaning in this motley collection of leftovers, but I doubt it. Dogs don't go in for symbolism much.

In the meantime, Elisha had become quite indispensable to Elijah, and showed promise of becoming a major prophet in his own right. Being ambitious in his own fashion, and knowing that he could learn a lot from the older man, Elisha stuck to him like a burr and, when Elijah sensed that his end was near and set off on a final farewell stroll from town to town, Elisha could not be dissuaded from following right along.

In fact, Elijah would have enjoyed some solitude for his few final days, but solitude is a luxury unavailable to prophets who are blessed with loyal apprentices. As they strolled and chatted, a chariot of fire appeared, with horses of fire, and a whirlwind dramatically whisked him away to heaven, where God was waiting to welcome him with balloons and a suitable celebration, no doubt.

After a decent period of mourning, Elisha rushed off to flex his miracle-making muscles in a broad variety of useful ways: producing fresh water and food during drought and famine, curing leprosy and barrenness, and even raising the dead. Soon Elisha was satisfied that he was every bit as good a prophet as Elijah had ever been. Maybe better.

Apparently miracles tended in those days to come in a fairly standard package, for all this sounds somewhat familiar. But supply does tend to follow demand, and these, admittedly, seem to be fairly universal problems. And, to be sure, the lack of creative design in miracle production did not make them any less impressive to the recipients.

No job was too large or too small, from floating a heavy axe head to healing a Syrian leper. He even dabbled in politics and international affairs.

It was this sideline that brought him to the attention of the king of Syria.

"Who's in charge of security?" demanded the Syrian king, after another in a long string of failed military forays. "It seems that every move the army makes these days is anticipated by the Israelites. There must be a spy in our midst. Who is he, and why has his blabbing mouth not been muzzled?"

The king's most trusted advisor stepped forward. "We've looked into this problem, sire. The leak seems to be through a pesky Israelite prophet named Elisha. He foresees our every move without ever even leaving the comfort of home."

"Well, blabbermouth prophets can be muzzled too. I want him brought here where I can see to it personally. Take a chunk of army and make it happen!"

Surrounded by a determined host of soldiers, Elisha was seized by a playful whim, and struck them all blind. Chaos ensued as the sightless troops fell all over each other quite helplessly.

"Well now," goaded Elisha. "Rather clumsy, for soldiers, aren't you? How on earth will you capture this Elisha fellow, wandering around in that state?"

"Don't be a smart-ass. We've been blinded...can't you tell? Who's speaking?"

"Well, I'm not Elisha, that's for sure. I'm some other guy. But I can lead you to Elisha, if you like," offered the wily prophet. As they could come up with no better way to search out their prey under the circumstances, the soldiers agreed to follow him.

After he'd led the stumbling men all the way into Samaria, he restored their sight—from a safe distance, of course—and enjoyed a good laugh at their expense.

"That's not funny, Elisha" said The Lord.

"Did you see the looks on their faces?" giggled Elisha

It was about this time that the king of Syria decided to besiege Samaria, which created a terrible famine. Prices soared astronomically, with asses' heads selling for eighty silver pieces, and even a quarter of a cab of dove's dung—that's a relatively small amount—costing five pieces of silver. (It's hard to translate these figures into modern currency...but try to remember the last time *you* paid five pieces of silver for a bit of dove's dung.)

As the king of Israel strolled along the city wall of Samaria, which was as close as he wanted to get to the common folk during such hard times, a woman called up to him for help. Always willing to interrupt his exercise for a worthy cause, he squatted down and listened to her story

"Well, sire," she said, "we're really hungry, you know, and the woman next door to me said, 'How about if we cook your son and eat him today. And then we can have my son for lunch tomorrow.' Well, it sounded like a reasonable arrangement. So we boiled my son with the last of the onions and a few greens, and he made a tasty dinner, if I do say so myself. Then, the next day, I called over to her and said 'We ought to get started braising your boy now, if he's to be tender by mealtime.' But she went and hid her son...and it's just not fair!"

The king, shredding his garments in grief, rushed off to blame Elisha for allowing all this to happen. The poor woman was left behind in confusion, watching the raggedy king scurry back along the wall and suspecting that he had somehow missed the main point of her story.

Now, it's difficult to see how Elisha could be blamed for all this, but that's what tends to happen when you set yourself up as the guy who fixes everything. In any case, he promised to fix this too.

"By this time tomorrow," he vowed, "the price of a measure of fine flour will be back to its pre-famine price: a shekel, no more, no less." He felt it was more discreet to use the price of flour as his benchmark, although it's clear that the price of dove's dung was of more concern to discriminating folk.

Everybody sat back and waited. Every one, that is, except for four lepers who sat starving outside the gate.

"It can't get much worse than this," groused one. "There's not a crumb left to be found in the city, and if there were, nobody's likely to rush out to share it with the likes of *us.*"

"You've got a point," agreed his fellow mendicant. "Our talents are being wasted here. Why don't we try sponging from the Syrian soldiers for a change?"

"Sure. What have we got to lose?"

Approaching the Syrian camp, they found it deserted. It appears that The Lord had made scary battle noises, and frightened them all away. Recognizing this as a piece of good luck, the lepers dined well on the food and wine that had been left behind, and carted away to some convenient hiding place several loads of gold and silver, as well as some particularly stylish clothes. Lepers were required to wear rags in those days, and they were sick of it!

Eventually, they thought to go back and break the good news to the king and the townspeople.

"The Syrians have gone," announced the lepers. "Just packed up and scuttled off home! And they've left a lot of good stuff behind."

"That's all very well," responded the king, suspiciously, "but how do I know this isn't simply a cleverly staged ambush?"

"Oh, yes indeed," jeered the frailest of the lepers. "There's a battalion of just such fit warriors as ourselves, hidden right outside the city gates, simply waiting for an appropriate opportunity to attack your troops. Well, suit yourselves. We've dined well today, and plan to go back for more."

The king was eventually persuaded to send a small force to check, and they found that, indeed, the siege was over.

Just as Elisha had promised, the price of flour immediately fell. (The price of dove's dung, incidentally, also returned to its accustomed moderate level, which was, indeed, a blessing for those who wanted some.)

While it's hard to say enough in praise of Elisha's contribution to the community, he could be somewhat peevish from time to time. As he approached Bethel on one of his miracle treks, the little children scampered out of the city, as children will, laughing and taunting him about his bald head. It must have been a sensitive issue for him. On impulse, he conjured two she-bears out of the woods and watched them tear the mischievous tykes to pieces. He probably regretted it afterwards.

King followed king in both Israel and Judah. God was never entirely satisfied with them, and apparently they weren't so very satisfied with him either, because their habit of searching for alternative deities verged on addiction. Nearing the end of his patience, He allowed the Assyrians to conquer Israel, carrying the people away into captivity...and the ten tribes of Israel were lost forever. Their cities were repopulated with strangers from strange lands who didn't even know Israel *had* a god. This didn't give The Lord the attention he craved, of course, but he had warned his chosen folks often enough and he had to teach them a lesson or risk losing face.

When Hezekiah became king of Judah, he pondered what had happened to Israel, and wondered whether God might be, in his subtle way, trying to tell them something. In an effort to improve his people's standing with The Lord, he pulled down as many of the heathen idols as he could conveniently get his hands on. He also noticed the deplorable condition of the temple. Rather than go to the trouble of maintaining it, the priests had simply turned off the lamps, locked the doors and wandered away. The king couldn't help feeling that a few of his more industrious women could put the place back in order and salvage much that appeared to be on the brink of destruction, but that was entirely out of the question. Women were forbidden here...which was probably how it had gotten in this condition in the first place. By the time he got a crew together to attend to it, much of the mess had to be thrown directly into the brook. But God appreciated the effort so when Judah was attacked by the Assyrians, he sent his most competent available angel to see what he could do to help. The angel, who was more efficient than creative, surreptitiously entered the Assyrian camp that very night and murdered nearly a hundred and eighty-five thousand of the soldiers.

This was, as it turned out, most effective in hampering their efforts. It would have worked well with almost any army of a similar size.

By the time Hezekiah's great-grandson Josiah became king at the age of eight, all the well-intentioned reforms and improvements had been largely forgotten, but Josiah had heard the old stories and wanted to follow in his ancestor's admirable footsteps. He was a precocious lad, and by the time he was eighteen, he had initiated a major renovation of the decaying temple, determined to restore it to its original glory. The workmen had barely started when one of the least of the priestly overseers found, tucked away on a back shelf among old accounting ledgers, the precious, the *original* Books of the Law! As thrilled as he was to view these sacred texts, Josiah also recognized their value as a propaganda tool in his ambitious attempt to herd the people back on track to the True Religion. He immediately whisked them into a prominent place of honour, and summoned the sage Huldah. She could always be relied on to give good advice, and he felt he could use a second opinion on how to exploit this windfall to best advantage.

A preliminary perusal of the Books revealed some excellent and practical ideas of a distinctly improving nature...but they were definitely not light entertainment. Huldah warned the boy that the people, having been accustomed over the years to much gaudier fare, would need some inducement to follow these more rigorous precepts.

"I think our best bet is to focus on guilt and fear," she suggested, "because rewards and persuasion have never seemed to work for any length of time. We may have to bend the truth a teeny bit, but it's in a good cause."

Gathering a wide selection of the most prominent people in Judah including the most senior of the priesthood, Josiah announced the re-discovery of the Books.

"They had just been pitched onto a dusty shelf, back behind the household accounts. I think the mice have been using them for...well, I'm sure you can imagine.

"My concern is that this oversight might cause some diplomatic problems with The Lord. I mean...I know they've been there a long time...it's not like we knew or anything...but who knows how he's going to feel about it. I mean, it could be considered...well ...disrespectful is not too strong a word. And he *has* tended to react rather badly when he felt insufficiently honoured. I have to tell you," he added, disarmingly, "I was tempted to simply tuck them back on the shelf and let one of my successors deal with the issue!"

Then he modestly relinquished the stage to Huldah, who would try to get a direct line to The Lord, and see exactly how bad the damage actually was.

After a few dramatic moments of silence, Huldah took on the demeanour of The Lord (she had to improvise a bit here) and bellowed, "How careless can you people *be*? You *mislaid* them? That's just insulting. You are going to be really sorry this time, and I'm not kidding!" The children of Israel saw that God had understood at once the implications of this *faux pas*, and was in no mood to cut them some slack.

Josiah and Huldah were worried that their little deception might have been too heavy-handed but in fact, it proved to be most effective. The people were frightened into compliance, at least long enough for Josiah to tear down the pagan altars that had been installed since his great-grandfather's time, and he even rooted out some of the old stuff Hezekiah had missed. At Huldah's suggestion, he drew on his obvious flair for drama to stage a Passover extravaganza, making up for lost time and demonstrating to the people that they, too, had a fun religion. Huldah herself was quite content to study the sacred books and occasionally fill in as a substitute teacher of the Laws.

The Lord must have seen the reforms of Hezekiah and Josiah as too little, too late. Nebuchadnezzar, king of Babylon, eventually attacked and besieged Jerusalem, carrying the Jews away into captivity and destroying the city, temple and all.

The Jews remained in captivity for seventy long years, until the Persians conquered Babylon and let them go. All this time, they may have neglected many of the other laws occasionally but they *always* remembered to rest on the Sabbath—so they were in pretty good shape to shoulder the temple treasures that the Persian king had generously allowed them to reclaim from the Assyrian loot stash, and trudge back to rebuild Jerusalem.

Chapter 10

Esther

When Persia conquered Babylon, the Jews who had been taken captive were free to return to their homeland. But many had made lives for themselves in the Persian territories, and not all scurried off the moment the opportunity was proffered.

The great Xerxes, king of Persia (Ahasuerus, to his friends) held a lavish feast at his favourite palace. He entertained all the time—of course he did—but this time he wanted to show everybody who was anybody how very much more important he was than they could ever hope to be. So he had the place dusted and polished, commandeered the best cooks and dancing girls, and sent out warm invitations to all the top nobles of Persia and Medea. No one declined what was shaping up to be the social event of the year.

The palace was breathtaking and the dancing girls, as always, were a huge hit. Relaxing after the lavish meal, the king graciously encouraged the men to feel comfortable. The wine flowed freely, but he insisted that they not feel obliged to drink if they felt disinclined...no, they could drink as much or as little as they pleased. It pleased them to drink a lot. The men got drunker and drunker and the party got noisier and noisier as they bragged about conquests in war and sports and candidly critiqued the afore-mentioned dancing girls.

Xerxes was quite tipsy by this time. “My queen Vashti,” he roared, “is so beautiful that she’d make them all look like second-rate goods by comparison!”

“Ho! Easy for you to say,” jeered his rowdy companions, “when she’s hidden away in the back somewhere. Bring her out and let us have a look.”

“No problem,” he hiccoughed, “...couldn’t be easier.” He sent a summons to the queen. “Tell her to get out here and dance for these, my best friends in all the world.” Tears filled his eyes as his thoughts lingered over their deep and abiding friendship, though the names of several eluded him just now.

In the queen’s apartments, Vashti lounged on silken cushions with the other wives, chattering gaily as they sampled rare sweets and sipped iced fruit juice, undisturbed by the sounds of rowdy brawling that intruded from the other end of the palace. When a servant arrived with the king’s summons, however, Vashti was seriously annoyed. She had no intention of being put on display like a dancing dog before a crowd of drunken louts. Sending her regrets, she explained that she was fully occupied entertaining her own guests.

She was hoping that Xerxes would be distracted by some other drunken tom-foolery and forget all about it.

By the time her reply was delivered, though, several of the king’s guests had downed enough liquid courage to bait the embarrassed king.

“All this luxury must have made you soft,” the boldest of them taunted. “We’re getting a little worried, buddy. How do you manage to rule half the civilized world? You can't even control your own wife!" And they all laughed.

Humiliated, Xerxes sent his chamberlains with orders to fetch her and this time, too proud to plead a sudden debilitating mystery illness (which would probably have been the most expedient option available to her), she refused outright. A damp blanket descended on the party and, seeking a scapegoat lest they be blamed, his guests whipped the king into a drunken rage.

"It's an insult," they muttered. "It's a rebellion! Our own devoted wives will be corrupted by the influence of the queen. They will begin to disrespect us...to despise us...and it'll be *all your fault.*" They worked themselves into a frenzy of rhetoric to brace up their sodden grievances.

"It's the king's *duty,*" they insisted, "to cast Vashti aside and choose another, a better wife."

Seeing now, with the clarity that comes only to the inebriated, the grave danger implicit in the queen's outrageous behaviour, Xerxes summoned a scribe and at once framed a decree:

"All wives must honour their husbands, no matter how undeserving, from the greatest noble to the lowest latrine-cleaner, and men must rule their wives."

The decree was sent out through all the land without delay, and the king and all the men felt proud and strong and very, very righteous.

The next day, as the effects of the carouse wore off and the king began to feel somewhat less righteous, he found himself dreading his next meeting with Vashti. She would be angry at being cast off—she was sure to tell him exactly what she thought of last night's fiasco—but he feared she wouldn't be nearly so heart-broken as his pride required. He warmed up to the idea of choosing a new wife. Vashti had a mind of her own...he wouldn't make *that* mistake again. This time he would find someone young—very young—and compliant...someone who would be grateful at being raised to such a high estate. And she must be beautiful. She must be more beautiful than Vashti.

"I'll hold a beauty contest," he decided. "And the successful entrant will win *me,* and will be queen over all Persia, as well!" Officers were immediately sent out to all corners of the land to choose contestants.

Competition for a place among these was fierce, but when the Jew Mordecai heard of the contest, he was sure he had a contender. He had raised his uncle's orphaned daughter since infancy, and she was a beauty! Calculating the favours that would come to him if Esther became queen, he feverishly groomed her for the event. He pawned everything he could spare to buy her a stylish and form-revealing robe, taught her to apply make-up in the latest mode (this required more skill than he had anticipated, but he did his best) and—most important—he warned her to, under *no* circumstances, mention that she was a Jew. He worried that this might not be seen as a positive attribute in the Persian palace.

One day, as he walked Esther unnecessarily close to the women's entry to the palace, hoping that she might catch the eye of Hegai, keeper of the women, the great man himself appeared in the courtyard. Thinking quickly, Mordecai pushed the girl, who stumbled to the ground under Hegai's feet, and the man tripped over her. As he picked himself up and dusted himself off, swearing not a little, he noticed her ever so slightly dusty beauty. Whisking her immediately into the women's apartments, he congratulated himself on his good fortune. Had it not been for this fortuitous accident, the king might have tripped over the clumsy girl himself one day and, noticing her beauty, wondered why Hegai wasn't doing his job as recruiter of local lovelies.

Barely more than a child, Esther waited in confusion to be paraded before the king. She was an obedient girl and had listened closely to Mordecai's instructions, but she scarcely understood what was required of her. And when her turn came, her innate modesty surfaced. Ignoring her uncle's tips on appropriate beauty pageant adornment, she asked for a simple linen gown, stuck a few pretty feathers in her hair and left her face free of all paint, even the interesting colours. Xerxes found her look rather refreshing, and chose her to join his stable of concubines as a finalist contestant. For the talent portion of the program, the king sampled the goods. Enthusiastically. Several times. Here was a girl who came when she was summoned and stayed until she was dismissed. She was obedient, beautiful, modest and young—very young. And her demeanour during their limited acquaintance suggested that she had no will of her own at all. The perfect wife! He declared Esther to be the winner.

Meanwhile, Mordecai spent every waking moment in the palace courtyard, eager to hear whether he had backed a winner. Miffed but undaunted when he wasn't invited to the wedding, he continued to linger around the king's gate, waiting to flag down Esther at some convenient moment with a sizable list of personal requests, and generally getting in everyone's way. Eventually, the palace attendants got used to the little toady hanging about and ignored him so completely that he was able to overhear a plot that threatened the king's life.

Certain of scoring major points this time, he found a way to get a message to Esther.

"Two of the king's chamberlains are plotting Xerxes' assassination," it read. "Warn him, and make sure he knows who to thank for the tip."

The plot was confirmed, and the two were hanged. But Esther had been too shy to mention her uncle, and no one important had noticed the little man who had spilled the beans, so his effort went unrewarded. Again.

At about this time, the Persian Haman was appointed Number One Prince. Everyone with any sense at all bowed and scraped before him, but since Mordecai thought Esther's position assured him a pipeline to the top, he did *not* bow. Neither did he scrape. And, hanging around by the gate there, he had plenty of opportunities. Unfortunately, while he had cautioned Esther not to mention that she was Jewish, he'd had a lot of time to kill in that courtyard and in the idler moments he'd regaled the servants at the gate with the story of his life in all its mundane details. One of those details was, of course, that he was a Jew.

The servants, who were thoroughly sick of seeing him underfoot all the time, now had the ammunition they needed. They went directly to Haman.

"You must have noticed the wretched little man who ignores your august self when you pass through the palace courtyard," began their designated spokesman. "We've all seen the insolent looks he casts your way, and it's a shame...such a noble, generous man as you are, sir...and always ready to reward any lowly, insignificant person who may be fortunate enough to do you some small service..."

"Yes, yes. Go on," prompted Haman.

"Well, he's not alone. We've found out that he's a Jew...his name's Mordecai...and that arrogant rudeness of his is just the first step in a dangerous program of social protest planned by the Jewish people."

Haman, still feeling insecure in his new position, was already enraged at Mordecai's lack of respect, and he was delighted to be offered an excuse to indulge his wrath on a truly majestic scale. He barely paused to toss a few coins to his helpful informants before scooting to the king with a warning.

"The Jews have initiated a Dangerous Social Protest" he said. "They disrespect your most Important Officials," he said. "They must be destroyed." he said. "Shall I make the arrangements?"

Xerxes didn't very much care. "Suit yourself." he mumbled, and he distractedly scribbled his signature on the decree Haman had jotted down on a handy scrap of papyrus while awaiting the king's attention. The decree set a date and time for the mass killing of the Jews in all provinces controlled by the Persian king, allowing an ample year for appropriate preparations.

Nobody thought to conceal these plans from the Jews themselves, so Mordecai appeared on the streets the next morning, clad dramatically in sackcloth with a top-dressing of ashes. Rushing to the palace, he demanded an immediate audience with Esther. Of course, the palace guards couldn't allow him to enter the building in that disreputable condition; they sent word to the queen that her uncle was at the gate, making a spectacle of himself. A little embarrassed, and still unfamiliar with palace protocol, Esther had to improvise, so she sent down some decent clothes and a chamberlain to ask "What's the problem?" In no time, the attendant was back with the rejected duds (she knew it wouldn't be that easy) and a copy of the offending decree, along with a demand that she address the matter with the king, and immediately! The frightened girl sent word to Mordecai: "You don't know how it is here. D'you think the king and I chat over morning coffee like we had something in common? If I approach him without being summoned, I'll be put to death! I'm not a diplomat...I'm just a beauty queen!"

Mordecai turned various colours with rage, and shook his fist at a random palace window. He didn't know which ones belonged to Esther, or he would have been more specific. "Don't think you'll escape this while the rest of us all perish, my girl. If you don't help us and The Lord has to step in to save the day, He's going to know where to find you, and you'll be in big trouble!"

"Right," muttered the harried chamberlain, "I'll tell her," and he trudged back over to the queen's chambers to deliver the message.

Poor little Esther was in a terrible state. The king still didn't know she was Jewish, and she didn't trust Mordecai not to tell, just out of spite. Warning him to keep out of the way—she didn't want him making it worse, whining and trailing ashes all about the place—she agreed to do what she could.

So what on earth *could* she do? Well, she had only been successful in one thing in all her young life—she'd won the beauty contest. So she came to the wise decision to go with her strength. She donned the simple linen gown Xerxes had seemed to like so much, searched the courtyard for a few stray feathers to stick in her hair and scrubbed her face really clean. Then she timidly entered the king's private courtyard, and stood quietly, hoping he would summon her to him. Fortunately, Xerxes was still infatuated with his meek young queen. Glancing up from whatever important thing he was doing at the time (he happened to be doing it with Haman) he noticed how charming she looked, standing there in that self-effacing way she had, and he beckoned to her.

"What can I do for you, my dear?" he asked. He was feeling generous. "Anything at all. The sky's the limit!"

Sensing that the sky would be of little use to her, she tried for something more modest. "I'd like to have a party tomorrow," she stammered "and I want you both to come. You and Haman. Nobody else. There!" They both agreed, smiling indulgently, and Esther scampered off, shedding feathers as she ran.

Haman was delighted. An invitation to a private shindig with the king and queen...he alone, of all the princes...it was a sign of extreme favour. His ego inflated until he was in danger of floating right out of the palace precincts. *Perhaps she fancies me,* he thought. *Why not? I'm a fine looking fellow!* And he rushed home to choose a suitable outfit for the occasion. As he checked to see whether his best robe needed cleaning, he thought: *Everything would be perfect if it weren't for that pesky, disrespectful Jew Mordecai.* He summoned the neighbourhood carpenter, and ordered a gallows to be constructed in his backyard immediately. *Tomorrow I'll hang him,* he thought. *Then I'll go to the party. What a great day!*

That night, the king couldn't get to sleep—perhaps he was excited about the party. As he lay in bed reading the fascinating chronicles of his reign, he came across the story of that assassination plot, and the little Jew who had foiled the dastardly scheme.

Calling the night-shift servants to him, he asked how Mordecai had been rewarded for this important service. The simple answer was...he hadn't been.

Well, it was late, but he was bored and he decided that he wanted to right this dreadful wrong at once, so he asked which of the senior officials was still within hailing distance. As luck would have it, Haman had been lingering around, hoping for an opportunity to ask permission to execute this same Mordecai. He was delighted to get the king's summons, and rushed right in.

"What do you suggest should be done to reward someone who has done a great service for a king?" asked Xerxes.

It must be me, thought Haman. *Who else?* He wondered what exceptional thing he had done for the king lately. No matter. There were so many to choose from. His mind began to race. "You might give him those embroidered ceremonial robes you wore at your wedding...the new ones you ordered will be delivered any day now anyway. And your second best horse. And you had a new crown made. You could give him the old one. (*Too much?* he wondered.) And...and...you could get someone important to deliver the things, on horseback...proclaiming through the streets: 'This is how the king treats those he wants to honour!' It would be a great public relations stunt."

"I can always count on you" murmured the king. He was starting to get sleepy. "You go find the stuff and deliver it all to Mordecai the Jew. And make sure you don't forget a single thing. Do it right now. Hurry. And turn down the lamps on your way out."

By the time the king's messengers came to escort him to Esther's banquet the next evening, Haman was in no mood for a party—he'd had a *really bad* day, and the night before had been no treat either. But attendance was not optional, and he arrived just in time to watch the king fawning over his dainty little wife, and saying to her yet again, "I wanted to bring you a special gift, but I couldn't think what you'd want? What can I give you? There must be something you'd like."

"Well," she lisped. "There is one teeny thing. I hate to ask. I'd like to live past my next birthday...if it isn't too much." She confessed to Xerxes that she was a Jew, and told him, as tactfully as she could, "It wouldn't be so bad if we were simply made slaves again...you're a great boss...but I understand that we're all going to be killed."

Xerxes was appalled. "Who's responsible for this outrage?" he roared. He ignored the fact that he himself must have signed the decree.

"Oh," responded Esther, pointing innocently at Haman, "it's definitely *him*. Definitely."

The king didn't trust himself to control his rage. Rather than frighten his delicate queen, he stalked out into the garden to invent an adequate punishment for the initiator of the dastardly decree.

In desperation, Haman dropped to his knees before the queen's couch and burst into tears. "I beg you, most abjectly...please intercede for my life!" He clutched her robes frantically.

Esther pulled away. "Get off me!" she shrilled. "You're getting tear stains on my party gown. And I think...oh, that's disgusting...you're drooling a little too!"

The king, having had a more rapid think than usual, strode back into the room at the most inconvenient possible time. Surprising Haman in mid-plea, he drew the conclusion kings almost always used to draw when coming upon such a scene. "Villain!" he cried. "...to choose such a time to force your attentions on my wife!" Haman immediately fainted dead away, but the king didn't require his input in order to choose a suitable punishment.

A word from Esther might have cleared up the misunderstanding but she was strangely silent. Even a beauty queen can hold a grudge.

As Xerxes wondered aloud what form of death would be most satisfying, a chamberlain who'd been waiting to serve the appetizers suggested, helpfully, "Well, I don't mean to be forward, but I know where there's a fresh gallows, put up just this morning...in a backyard, just around the corner."

"Fine," said the king. "Hang him, then." So they did.

Having gotten this out of the way, Xerxes promptly lost interest in the whole extermination issue. He summoned Mordecai to deal with the matter on his behalf. "Reverse the decree. Write whatever you like. Seal it yourself...here's my ring. Wait...you'll need to be paid for your trouble. I know...take Haman's house. I think it's just around the corner. You can have his stuff too. Tell them I said so."

The decree Mordecai sent out ordered that all Jews in the country were to be allowed to kill and plunder anyone who had done them wrong, including women and children, though it's hard to know how the children might have caused offence. On the same day that the extermination of the Jewish people had been planned, the Jews had a murder-fest, killing everyone who had so much as given them a dirty look. Seventy-five thousand people were slaughtered in the land that day...five hundred in the palace alone. Then the Jewish people celebrated with a big banquet, where Mordecai was honoured as Xerxes' right hand man, and a great peacemaker to boot.

Esther attended the feast with the others, but she felt bad for the small children. They'd never done *her* any harm.

Chapter 11

Job

A very long time ago, in the land of Uz, there lived a man named Job, who took a great pride in being ever so good and righteous, always obeying God's law and avoiding evil as if it had a foul odour. His vigilant quest to root out even the tiniest pocket of evil in order to step around it with distaste was almost obsessive. It was not easy being married to such a man.

Over the years, God had made Job the richest man in the district, with many oxen and she-asses, and even more sheep and camels, all of which Job accepted placidly as a fitting reward for loyal service. He and his wife had also been favoured with seven strapping sons and three beautiful daughters although his fastidiousness had extended to limiting himself modestly to one wife only...and no concubines at all. Mrs. J. appreciated that—really, she did. But it meant that she'd had to pump out every one of those babies herself, single-handedly. (Well, she'd actually had two hands available...but they hadn't been a lot of help.)

As his charming family grew, they developed private, happy traditions that often, oddly, did not include their upright father. Each son, for instance, on his birthday, would arrange a celebration feast in his own house and the brothers and sisters would eat and drink gaily together in the most companionable way. Job would always spend these days making compensatory burnt offerings to The Lord, on the off chance that the carousals might cause the revellers to stumble into some sin or other. Mrs. J usually arranged to sneak off while the offerings were burning to join the young folks for an hour or two of innocent family fun, and sometimes caught herself disloyally wondering whether he wasn't being a bit of a sanctimonious ass.

During a break in one of God's periodic business meetings with Satan—they still got together regularly in those days—he mentioned, complacently, "How about that guy Job! He's so good and righteous...and he's totally devoted to me. That must really bug you. Have you noticed how he avoids evil?"

"Yeah," snorted Satan. "I've noticed. He walks around all the time with a look on his face like somebody in his vicinity passed wind. It's very annoying. Anyway, it's no big wonder that he worships you. Look at all the stuff you've given him. He lives like a king! Take away some of that stuff, and see how he feels *then*. He'll turn on you soon enough."

"Oh, you're just jealous," said The Lord. "Go ahead and do what you want to his stuff, and we'll see. But don't hurt him."

The next day, a messenger approached Job.

"The Sabeans have stolen all your oxen and she-asses, and killed all your servants," he blurted. "Only I managed to escape, just so I could tell you." Job didn't recognize the man, but then, he had a great number of servants and couldn't be expected to know them all at a glance.

Within minutes, another messenger burst in. "Some kind of strange fire from out of the heavens has burnt up all the sheep as well as the shepherds who were tending them. Only I escaped...on purpose...so I could tell you about it." Job didn't recognize him either, but he was clearly a little singed around the edges, which gave his story a certain credibility.

Hot on his heels, a third messenger arrived. "The Chaldeans stole every one of the camels and killed the servants..."

"I know, I know," snapped Job. "You managed to sneak away so you could tell me." He was becoming irritable, and found it hard to receive the man's news with a becoming degree of good grace. "Thanks." The man seemed, once again, unfamiliar to him, but he had clearly been running and was out of breath, so Job refrained from questioning him further.

As he ushered him out the door, yet another messenger was awaiting his turn. "I have some really bad news for you," he gasped, choking on the cloud of dust that rose from his garments whenever he moved. "Your eldest son was entertaining his brothers and sisters today. It was his birthday, you know..."

"Oh, my extreme goodness," interjected Job. "I completely forgot. I should be burning offerings in case they are misbehaving in some obscure way."

"Yeah, well..." coughed the man, "a freak wind blew the house down, and it fell on them and killed them all...every last one. I managed to crawl out of the rubble, solely in order to rush over and tell you about it."

This time, Job didn't even *try* to recognize the guy. He detected a disturbing pattern emerging here, and began to wonder whether God might be punishing him for something. It couldn't have been anything *he* had done, of course. Perhaps, then, for something somebody else had done. *Oh, well,* he thought, resignedly *...The Lord giveth and The Lord taketh away.* After pondering this and praying for a while, he tore up his clothes a bit, shaved his head, and threw himself down on the ground in a paroxysm of grief over the untimely death of his dear children. Later in the evening, he thought to send one of his remaining servants to Mrs. J. with the bad news.

The next time that God and Satan chatted, The Lord couldn't resist the urge to gloat, just a little. "Well, what do you think of Job now? You see! Even though we've taken away almost everything he had—good work, by the way—he still doesn't blame me. He's quite as devoted as ever. Admit it...you were wrong on this one."

"Well," conceded Satan, "I'll admit that I was surprised. But so far, we haven't really *hurt* him. All the real pain has fallen on somebody else. Perhaps if he'd been in that house with his kids...but it's too late for that. I'm telling you, put him in some actual discomfort and you'll hear him hum a different hymn."

Satan knew The Lord couldn't resist a sporting challenge. "OK, then," God agreed. "You can hurt him if you like. But don't kill him. If you kill him, all bets are off."

Before the week was out, Job was covered with boils from head to toe. Sometimes they itched and sometimes they stung, and he couldn't decide which was worse. When he couldn't stand the itching one moment more, he scraped away at his skin with a shard of broken crockery, but that merely opened the sores and left him in agony. Finally, he spent most of his time sitting in the ash heap, hoping to get some relief.

It's hard to imagine how he expected that to help ...perhaps the notion was just another of Satan's little jests.

"Get out of the ash heap this minute," insisted Mrs. J. "You have to come in for meals eventually, and you're going to track that stuff all over the house."

"Listen," she said, "this is one really nasty affliction. It looks like God definitely has it in for you...and you've been so righteous," (...*to a fault,* she thought). "It doesn't seem fair."

"No, no," he protested mildly, attempting a suitably beatific smile. "Shame on you! The Lord has given us many good things over the years. Now he sees fit to test my devotion. It's my duty to accept these things with a loving spirit. I'm much, much too pious a person to complain."

"Fine," she said, rolling her eyes. "Better you than me."

But it wasn't *much* better. By the time a few of his friends dropped in to visit, he was getting whiney and she welcomed the break. "He has an affliction, fellows," she told them. "He's feeling pretty sorry for himself right now, so see what you can do to cheer him up." She ushered them into the back room where Job was moping the day away.

It took a few minutes for their eyes to adjust from the summer sunlight, and even then they could barely recognize him. "Wow!" they exclaimed, sympathetically. "You're a mess. What happened?" By this time, Job's face was a mass of running boils and his eyes were nearly swollen shut. Their sensitive reaction to his plight opened the floodgates of his self-pity, and he cursed the moment he had been born. Hinting that a national day of mourning might be held on his birth-date, he expressed regret that his old mother was not still available to accept her share of the guilty responsibility, for bringing him into the world at all. As they backed toward the door, Mrs. J. intercepted them with a huge tray of tasty nibbles. She was an excellent cook, and everybody knew it. They couldn't resist, so they stayed a while longer.

"We came over to distract you for a while," they claimed, edging as far from their sick friend as they could get without leaving the room altogether. "Let's have a cold drink and some snacks, and debate God's intention in all this. It'll be like old times."

"Well, I haven't been able to do a whole lot lately besides think about it," said Job "and I've been wondering whether justice fits into His plan at all! I've always been so very careful to do what He wants. I prayed. I burned offerings. Perhaps He doesn't actually go out of his way to favour the Really Righteous. Maybe he simply treats everybody (here he shuddered a little) the same! I mean...what's the point of being good all the time if you're going to be punished anyway?"

"Did you ever think," suggested one of his friends, "that maybe you're not quite as good as you think you are?"

"Yeah," offered another, "I have to tell you...you're just not that good." He was obviously remembering the many times Job had offered them unsolicited advice on self-improvement. "Maybe you should be *glad* The Lord is taking the trouble to correct you. Perhaps all this..." he waved his hand vaguely in Job's direction, "is a character-building exercise."

"Oh, sure," complained Job, scratching himself. "Easy for *you* to say. This is horrible. I'd rather be dead. I toss and turn...and just when I think it's getting better, it breaks out again. Nobody ever had to go through anything like this before...*ever.* I hurt and I itch...and I smell!"

"Yeh, yeh...we noticed," they muttered.

"My wife won't sleep with me anymore...not even to replace those kids I lost in the fire. There were nine or ten of them at one time, I think. And urchins make fun of me when I go out in the street. I'm disgusting!

"Yeh, yeh...we noticed." More muttering.

"You know," said Job, "you're no help at all. You could be a whole lot more sympathetic. I could dole out cheap advice and criticism, too, if you were in my place...but no! I'd try to think of nice, comforting, supportive things to say. *That's* how good *I* am."

They suspected that the afternoon wasn't going as well as they had intended. "Who can figure out God?" they offered. "Perhaps you did some little thing... or committed some tiny error of omission. Maybe if you tried just bit harder..."

"Who are you to tell me that?" Job snapped. "I'm *so much* better than all of you. And I always have been."

There seemed to be little point in continuing the discussion. And the snacks were almost gone. In any case, his sores seemed to ease only when he was wallowing in the mire of his own righteousness; their lack of worthiness could only serve to irritate him. On their way out they passed his wife, looking much as though she had heard it all before.

If Mrs. J. thought the afternoon's discussion had worn out her husband's interest in the topic of his misery, she was sadly mistaken. Dinner was barely started when he pushed aside his plate and blurted, "If I could only get a chance to sit down with God and remind Him of all the ways I've served Him, I'm sure He would reconsider. I never think of myself...you know that. If I could reason with Him...if He only realized..." He called for writing materials and began at once listing all the people who were not *nearly* so devout as he was, carefully tabulating the details of their transgressions. He had been watching carefully, and was pretty sure he could remember every last one.

His wife finished her meal and began to clear the table. He continued to scribble. "You know," she blurted, in exasperation, "You need to find a hobby. What's the use of all that? The Lord's not going to bother justifying himself to *you*."

It was a sobering thought. He pushed the list aside for the moment, although she noticed that he later folded it carefully and tucked it away in a convenient spot, just in case.

"Perhaps you're right," he said. "I guess I'll simply have to continue suffering with pious resignation, and trust that God will eventually remove this tribulation." And raising his eyes to where the heavens would be if there weren't a ceiling in the way, he couldn't resist adding, "...and the sooner, the better."

That night, as Job lay dozing and squirming uncomfortably in his bed, God appeared to him in a fitful dream. Without preamble, He stated, "I'm getting fed up with your attempts to figure me out. Forget it. You think you're so smart? Where were you when I was creating the world? That was a big job...I could've used some help. You couldn't begin to do the stuff I've done...not on your best day! You don't need to understand where I'm going with these things. You just need to obey. Do we understand each other?"

Job stared in awe and terror then scrambled to his knees. "I'm a vile wretch," He agreed. "I'm a worm! I can't apologize enough for the very few tiny things I must have inadvertently done wrong. How could I presume to question your judgment?"

"You're not kidding," said The Lord. "I have more important things to do than explain myself to *you*. You think you deserve better? What have you ever given me that you think I owe you anything?"

"I see that now," said Job, in his most conciliatory manner. "I do. And I appreciate you taking the trouble to drop by. I feel bad bothering you about all this. But as you're here..." he added, pulling the list he had compiled out from under his pillow, "you might want to have a look at this list of people who deserve these afflictions a whole lot more than I do."

"Well," said The Lord, "maybe just a glance." He glanced. "All right," he said. "I'm convinced."

"I knew you would be," murmured Job modestly.

He awoke the next morning feeling ever so much better. And, in fact, before too long, his fortunes improved and he became even richer than ever before. His skin condition cleared up, and he indicated a desire to replace the children he had lost in that unfortunate fire. Mrs. Job was relieved that things were going better for him, but this is where she drew the line. She indicated to him, in no uncertain terms, that he'd better stretch his moral code around the idea of acquiring at least one more wife to take on the child-bearing responsibilities—she had done enough! He felt he could make this concession, so she found him a much younger wife or two and in no time, all seven of his sons as well as the three daughters were replaced by others almost as strapping and beautiful as the originals.

Job accepted all this good fortune graciously, as barely adequate repayment for his outstanding patience under adversity.

"Just great!' grumbled Satan, when he next met with The Lord. "Now he's sure to be even more annoying than ever." And he was.

Chapter 12

Daniel

The Babylonians didn't rise to the top of the heap without an effective program to foster and encourage excellence, and they saw no reason why the Jews captive in their midst shouldn't benefit from that program. So the brightest and the best of the children of Israel were selected to live and be educated in the King's palace.

As part of an effort to render their residence homier, the pupils were fed dishes from the king's own table. But pleasing these lads was a challenge fraught with pitfalls. The complex dietary laws of the Jews were quite unfamiliar to the Babylonians.

"We can't eat this stuff!" protested Daniel, who had appointed himself leader of the boys. "I'm sure you mean well, but *we* would consider ourselves defiled by the consumption of even so much as a single *crumb* of your king's meat.

"I, myself," he insisted, fastidiously, "will eat only pulse, cooked plain."

"Pulse!" cried the palace kitchen staff, "Pulse is for peasants. We never serve *pulse!"*

The prince of the eunuchs, who was responsible for the condition of the boys, agreed to an experiment. David and three of his staunchest supporters were allowed to eat only pulse and water while it was insisted that the rest of the students overcome their distaste and choke down the delicately seasoned meats prepared for the king, whether they liked it or not.

At the end of the ten days, Daniel and his pals appeared to have grown even fatter and sleeker than the others. The resourceful prince of eunuchs promptly gave orders that all of the Jewish boys were to be put on a strict diet of pulse and water, and discreetly found a profitable market for their share of the royal meals outside the palace confines.

While Daniel gloated visibly, his popularity among the boys showed a marked decline and it's not entirely certain that all were equally enthusiastic over the results of this particular theological triumph. Nevertheless, as his education progressed, Daniel's confidence grew, and he impatiently awaited an opportunity to display his many stellar attributes before those who could do him the most good.

One night, King Nebuchadnezzar awoke with the impression that he had dreamed a most intriguing dream. Calling for his astrologers and sorcerers, he demanded an interpretation.

"I've had a most intriguing dream," he stated, loudly. (They were rather a large crowd.) "Which of you would prefer to give me the interpretation? Don't all press forward at once."

There was, nevertheless, some jostling for position, and at least a dozen voices asked, eagerly, "What was the dream, your Exaltedness?"

"I can't remember...I guess you'll have to tell me that too. Who's up for it? There'll be a substantial reward for the winner."

The crowd rippled as eager front-liners attempted to fade back into the group. "But that's impossible," murmured a few. "Only the gods could do such a thing. He *has* to tell us the dream. Those are the rules!"

"You're just stalling," snapped Nebuchadnezzar. "I don't have to do any such thing. Now, let me hear some suggestions...and don't get it wrong or I'll have you all cut up into tiny pieces and your homes remodelled into dunghills. So, who's first?"

Daniel, who happened to be studying astrology that day, was among those present. He recognized the sound of opportunity beating at his door and hastened to respond. "Oh...oh...I know that one..." he said. "Pick me!"

"Fine, fine...whoever. Just spit it out," demanded the impatient king.

"You dreamed," said Daniel, confidently, "of a great image of gold and silver, brass and iron. The feet were made of clay and a big rock dropped onto its toes, smashing them to bits. Then the whole statue crumbled to dust and blew away in the wind." He realized that it wasn't the most dramatic of dreams...but it was all he could come up with on the spur of the moment, and he was determined to do better with the interpretation.

He went on. "And it means—no offence—that our all-powerful Hebrew God is going to destroy your mighty kingdom, feet first."

This dream image must have sounded at least vaguely familiar to the impressionable king because Daniel was immediately appointed ruler of the entire province and chief governor over all the wise men in the kingdom. It was so much easier to get on the fast track in those days—although it clearly could involve a certain element of risk, and required a bold and enterprising manner.

As his first official act, he pulled strings to obtain plum posts in the province for his three loyal sidekicks, whose Hebrew names had been changed to Shadrach, Meshach and Abednego for the convenience of their Babylonian masters.

Apparently, kings in those days had very short memories, because in no time at all, Nebuchadnezzar was concocting a new scheme for civic improvement, showing no regard whatsoever for the dream-threats of the Jewish deity.

"This time," he told his Minister of Culture, "I've come up with something really unique. I don't know why you didn't think of it yourself.

"I want you to commission an impressive golden image to be set up in some appropriately conspicuous public place."

The Minister smiled politely, and waited.

"But that's not all. I want everyone to drop instantly to the ground in an abjectly grovelling stance to worship it whenever any music is heard...any music at all. Don't you love it?"

"Inspired!" gushed the Minister. "I'll see to it immediately." And he did.

It became a major pain in the hind quarters because zealous royal enforcers chose to interpret the order to cover even casual, music-like sounds: a hummed tune would suffice. The people made every effort to comply, since those who failed to do so were immediately thrown into a fiery furnace to meditate on their bad manners. But the hard of hearing and even the tone deaf were at a distinct disadvantage, and hearing aids of every variety were soon in high demand.

Before long, complaints began to surface against the children of Israel, who had been expressly forbidden by their God to worship any such images—regardless of music, whatever the tune. Predictably, the focus of attention fell on Shadrach, Meshach and Abednego, whose easy rise on the coattails of Daniel had been widely noted and deeply resented.

When they were first brought before the king, he attempted to make excuses on their behalf for Daniel's sake. "Maybe you misunderstood the decree," the king suggested, "what with the unfamiliar language and all..."

But the three young men were not at all inclined to accept this loophole graciously.

"No, there was no misunderstanding," they declared. "We just don't do that kind of thing."

"Well," threatened Nebuchadnezzar, "how do you feel about crisping up in the furnace?"

"Oh, that'll never happen," they explained, breezily. "Our God is sure to protect us from the flames...we can do pretty much as we please as long as we don't break *his* rules. We already explained all this to the guards. Can we go now?"

"I don't think so," snapped the king, seriously offended that his gesture of leniency had been rejected so cavalierly. "We're going to put that theory to the test.

"Guards, shut them in the furnace," he commanded, "and let's increase the heat sevenfold, to make it interesting." This was a bit of theatrical overkill be-cause after all, fried is fried, and anything more is just sizzle.

As the Jews were securely bound and cast into the furnace fully dressed, attendant soldiers standing injudiciously close to the fire began to burst into flame and burned rapidly to charred cinders. The three Jews, on the other hand, fell to their knees and belted out a bracing hymn in praise of their God, who must have been hovering conveniently nearby, waiting to be of service. By the time the king had relocated his chair a safer distance from the action, the fetters binding the men had burned off and he could see them strolling about in the flames accompanied by what looked very much like an angel.

Now, Nebuchadnezzar had always rather wanted to meet an angel, so he promptly called everyone out of the furnace, and lined them all up to have a good look. Except for a small hole burnt in the sleeve of one and a scorched bit on the sandal of another, not one of the Jews was even singed. The angel had disappeared in a puff of smoke, but the king managed to swallow his disappointment. He was still sufficiently impressed with the performance to promote the three men to even loftier positions than before.

"And furthermore," he commanded, "I don't want to hear another word spoken against their god. We can't be sure what other tricks he may have up his sleeve. Anyone who disobeys this prohibition is to be cut into little pieces...and their houses are immediately to be converted into dunghills."

This was one of the king's favourite punishments. The city was becoming dotted with dunghills. In some places, they were so numerous as to create a serious health hazard.

After his death, Nebuchadnezzar's son Belshazzar became king. Determined not to be overshadowed by his quirky father, he became quite the party animal. His entertainments became more and more lavish, until one day—it might have been his birthday—he invited a thousand of his favourite lords with their wives and concubines to a great feast. After the invitations went out, he realized that he didn't have enough 'best' wine goblets to serve the lot. It was too late to trim down the guest list, so he decided to get creative and brought out the gold and silver vessels that had been filched years ago from the temple in Jerusalem, judging that they should do very well for toasting the native Babylonian gods.

He meant no disrespect, and the beautifully wrought vessels were highly praised by his guests. But anyone familiar with the delicate sensibilities of the Jewish God would have known that this gaff would not go unnoticed. As the king sat sipping his wine, an annoying buzz of comments from nearby guests drew his attention to the wall behind him, where the fingers of an eerily disembodied hand were busily defacing the plaster surface with cryptic graffiti. Thankful that the folds of his robe concealed the knocking of his knees, the terrified king summoned his astrologers and soothsayers and demanded an immediate explanation. Unfortunately, the official magicians were unable to read the mysterious words, leaving the unenlightened king positively quaking in fear (by this time, it was clearly apparent to the most casual observer). Someone must have run to tell the queen, who had been quietly reading in her chambers and trying to ignore the din from the festivities, for she strode irritably into the banquet house and up to the defaced wall. She was a fair scholar but the script was unfamiliar to her, and it was clear that the cowering astrologers and soothsayers had been no use at all—as usual. A glance at the trembling king was enough to show her that he would be quite helpless until this mystery was solved.

She sat down beside him, keeping well clear of his uncontrollably trembling knees. "I seem to remember reading about some problem your father had, several years ago, getting these useless magicians to interpret a dream." She said. "There was a fellow who was rather helpful at the time...I think his name was Daniel. He was appointed Master of Magicians, Primary Dream Interpreter and Major Dissolver of All Doubts...or some such thing. I don't suppose anyone thought of summoning him?"

Of course, no one had.

By the time Daniel arrived, the king was ready to promise him anything at all if only he could translate the message. Daniel noted the king's agitation with distaste.

"Keep your rewards," he said. "I don't do contract work any more. But I'll have a look at it...as a favour." The queen raised her eyebrows, sceptically.

He examined the words on the wall. They read:

"Mene, Mene, Tekel, Upharsen."

He nodded wisely, and assured the king that the hand bits had clearly been sent by The Lord, who had conveyed this message as a warning to the Babylonians. He proceeded with the translation:

"Mene...that means 'God has numbered thy kingdom and finished it'."

The guests stirred uncomfortably.

"Tekel...that means 'you have been weighed in the balance and found wanting'."

The king managed to look offended, despite the knocking of his knees.

"Peres...that means 'your kingdom will be divided and given to the Medes and Persians.'"

"Wait a minute!" commanded the queen. "Didn't you say the last word was Upharsen?"

"No," snapped Daniel. "I said "Peres."

"I'm sure I heard you say Upharsen," insisted the queen.

"Well, it's the same word, anyway," mumbled Daniel irritably. "Peres is the passive participle."

"Fine," returned the queen, "I was just checking."

"Medes and Persians, eh?" said the king, dragging together the shreds of his dignity, "That doesn't sound good...not good at all...but I suppose it's as well to be warned. We'll work out a defence plan first thing tomorrow morning."

On his way to bed, Belshazzar rewarded Daniel with a handsome red suit and a costly gold chain which (the queen noted, wryly) the prophet accepted despite his earlier show of resistance. Daniel was also promoted to an even more exalted position than ever ...which didn't count for much, because that night Belshazzar was killed and the Persian King Darius conquered Babylon.

Daniel certainly seemed to have a peculiarly winning way with kings of all persuasions. Before long and for no very apparent reason, Darius developed a burning desire to make Daniel number one president over the whole kingdom. Naturally, the other presidents and princes, many of whom had toadied and manoeuvred years and years before attaining their positions of prominence, became jealous. They were further frustrated by their inability to find in him any fault with which to besmirch him in the eyes of the monarch.

As they hung around the pool grousing in one of the princely courtyards, one prince's favourite concubine —she never left his side—interjected:

"Surely you can find a way to trick Darius into getting rid of this Daniel fellow!"

Her particular prince patted her buttocks fondly. "It's no use. He likes Daniel. He'd change his mind after a bit. He does it all the time."

"But isn't there some old law about written decrees ...they can't just be changed like that, can they?" She tried to look as if she didn't know the answer to this question already. She wasn't new at this concubine game, and she always kept her ears open.

"Well...no," answered the prince. "Once a decree is signed, it can't be changed. The gods don't like it. I think it's something about the papyrus—or the ink—I don't know." He popped another fig into his mouth and took a sip of wine.

"Give me until tomorrow," she said. "I'll think of something." She didn't like Daniel. He always made her feel underdressed.

The next day, the princes and presidents—except for Daniel, of course—went, in a body, to speak to Darius. "We've noticed that there haven't been a lot of people hanging around the palace lately, petitioning you for favours. We understand they're addressing all the smaller issues to their own gods"

"...and I couldn't be more delighted," claimed Darius. He was trying to get some administrative details cleared up to make time for a stroll in the garden before dinner. "Saves me listening to all their tedious requests. People are so petty."

"But shouldn't *you* be the one to decide which favours to grant? After all...who can keep track of the subversive agendas of all these foreign deities? And doesn't it show a certain lack of respect...?"

"Oh. Well. I guess I hadn't thought of it quite that way. What do you suggest?"

"Well, we've taken the liberty to draft a decree stating that anyone who asks a petition of any god or man other than yourself will be cast into the nearest den of lions. It's only for ninety days, for starters. We can always revise it later if it isn't working out. Just sign here..."

Darius reluctantly scratched his name onto the decree. As if there weren't enough petty chores interrupting his day already!

Thereafter, there was rarely a night when one prince or president or another wasn't to be found peeping in through Daniel's window, waiting to spot a transgression. It wasn't long before the devout prophet was spotted at his evening prayers. Darius was immediately informed, and the nearest available lion's den was made ready to receive an additional occupant. The king felt bad about it, and would have saved Daniel if he could. But there was no denying the royal signature scrawled on the bottom of that decree.

The next morning, Daniel was pitched headlong into the lion's den. (It was more of a pit, really, but it did house a lion—and rather a big one at that.) Daniel looked briefly into the fierce eyes of the ravenous animal and fell to his knees.

Speaking as rapidly as he could without blurring his words, he begged The Lord to help him in his extreme need. "You needn't come yourself, if it's inconvenient," he chattered. The lion slunk closer, licking its lips. "That angel—the one in the furnace—he'd do fine. Just tell him to rush...please!"

When Darius' morning constitutional took him near the den, he sauntered over and shouted down, "Daniel! You still there?"

"Of course," replied the familiar voice of the prophet. "Where would I be?"

"Your god saved you, then?"

"Well, I'm answering you, aren't I?"

Darius had to admit that he had a point. "Where's the lion?"

"There was this angel— he's gone now— he wrestled the lion's mouth shut. It was quite a struggle. The lion's exhausted, I guess. He's sleeping...hey, are you going to let me out of here, or what?"

"An angel? You don't say! I'm sorry I missed him. Sure...you can come out."

On the king's orders, the entrance to the den was unsealed and Daniel strolled out. (Actually, he climbed out...but he did it so nonchalantly that it looked like a stroll.) As soon as he got home, he sent over a couple of juicy big steaks for the lion, to show there were no hard feelings.

Kings' whims being what they are, he thought, *there's no sense being bad friends with a hungry lion.*

Chapter 13

Susanna

For much of the Babylonian captivity, many of the Jews lived in a manner very nearly approaching normal. They transacted business, enforcing their own particular laws within their own communities and their status as captives allowed them to indulge in a certain pleasant informality when it came to courtroom arrangements.

It seemed natural that people should gravitate to the spacious walled garden of the wealthy Joacim whenever it became necessary to address lawsuits and other sticky issues of governance. And Joacim was glad to oblige. In fact, he was flattered...for a while. But soon there were people milling about all day, every day. It was way too much of a good thing. Joacim began shooing the riff-raff out by noon so that his beautiful wife Susanna could relax among her flowers with some assurance of privacy.

It was more difficult to find a tactful way to oust the more senior members of the community, and a couple of the ancient judges developed an inconsiderate inclination to dawdle about, using their feeble health as an excuse to linger...hoping for an illicit glimpse of the lovely lady of the house.

It became a guilty secret habit, then a veritable obsession, which each hid from the other and from all the world as well. Nothing could be more ridiculous than the antics of these two old rakes, sneaking around behind the trees and peeping out from the bushes until all hours of the afternoon. It was inevitable that they should eventually discover the presence of one another, as neither was terribly agile.

"Oh, do pardon me," whispered the clumsier of the two. "I'm afraid I didn't notice you, crouched in the underbrush here. I was, um, searching for, um, something small that I lost here...sometime."

"Yes, well..." murmured his colleague irritably, easing his hand from under the other's sandal, "It's not here. I would have noticed. Anyway, I was just on my way home. For dinner."

"Dinner. Yes. As was I." And they hobbled off in separate directions, stopping to eye each other suspiciously every few yards or so.

As soon as they were hidden by the lush foliage, they each snuck back through the bushes to the same spot, which was an ideal vantage point from which to wait for a peek at the unsuspecting Susanna. When they stumbled over each other once more within five minutes of parting, there appeared to be no further use in attempting to hide their motives from one another. The two huddled there amongst the fallen leaves and the caterpillars, confessing their lustful passions and plotting to surprise the object of their affections sometime when she would be alone and vulnerable.

They didn't have long to wait. On one hot, humid afternoon, after everyone had appeared to leave the garden and she believed she was quite alone with her maids, Susanna decided to refresh herself by bathing in a suitably secluded fountain. She sent her attendants off for the necessary bath accoutrements and to ensure her privacy by shutting the garden gates. Recognizing an opportunity that might not come again, her two besotted admirers hauled their creaky limbs out of the shrubbery and confronted their startled hostess.

"Have pity on us," whined one decrepit intruder. (I don't know which one it was. They were pretty much interchangeable.) "We've snuck around here for days and days, watching you. We adore you...you're so beautiful. Any chance you'd lie with us right here on the grass? What do you say?"

Susanna snatched her robe away from their groping fingers in disgust. "You're kidding," she spat. "Get away from me!"

Astutely realizing that they would have little hope of overpowering their prey, and suspecting that she might not submit to them willingly, the two old rakes had already settled on threats as the most effective strategy available to them.

"Look," they warned, "if you don't give us what we want, we'll denounce you. We'll say we caught you here with a young lover. Everyone will believe it...there are two of us, and we're really old! You won't have a chance; you'll lose everything. Think it over."

She thought it over...for a breath. With her next breath, she screamed for help.

The two old profligates had formulated a contingency plan to cover this very possibility. As one scrambled to open the garden gate, the other clutched the arm of the struggling woman and struck a pose, incorporating as much dignity as the situation allowed.

By the time her servants ran into the garden to her defence, both elders were berating Susanna indignantly: "Whore! Harlot! Shame, shame on you..." and much more in a generally similar tone.

Neither the distinguished position of the two intruders, nor their rehearsed protestations deterred

Susanna's loyal attendants from ejecting them summarily from the property; they had never seen or heard anything at all suspicious in their mistress's demeanour and believed, one and all, in her complete innocence. Susanna, nevertheless, had to nurse her outrage alone. Her husband spent the night nervously weighing the politics of accusing two respected judges of such blatantly despicable behaviour.

The next day, however, when the people assembled in Joacim's garden as usual, he was shocked to hear the tables turned as the two unrepentant culprits accused Susanna of adultery and demanded that she be put to death. The rejected lovers had decided that this would be the most efficient way to remove all evidence of what they now agreed was a potentially embarrassing misadventure.

"We were just lingering in the garden, enjoying the heat of the sun on our poor rheumatic old bones, when the lady appeared. Having no wish to intrude, we retreated considerately into the bushes near an isolated fountain where we heard her send her maids away, admonishing them to make sure the gates were shut...a little furtively, we thought. As we waited for a discreet opportunity to retreat, a young man stepped out of the bushes and swept her into his arms. She had clearly been expecting him, the hussy, for they sank down right there on the grass and began fondling each other in the most intimate way.

"As soon as we had seen enough to be very, very sure what they were up to— oh, it was most distressing— we rushed out to put a stop to the wickedness! With complete disregard for our own safety, we threw ourselves on the man, but we couldn't hold the brute...he was too strong. He wrenched himself away and fled out of the garden gate. We somehow managed to hold on to this shameless woman until help came.

"We'll swear to all this and we insist that she be immediately executed for the lewd and sinful trollop she is...and the sooner the better."

A hush fell over the assembly. All eyes turned toward Susanna and a sympathetic murmur spontaneously rippled through the crowd:

"Oh...well...what a shame to have to put her to death. But it can't be helped. It'll be so hard on her family. And she's so pretty!"

Susanna leapt to her feet. "That's *it?"* she asked, in shock. "You're *done?"*

"Well...the old guys say..."

She saw that her poor womanly protestations of innocence would weigh not at all against the testimony of the two men.

"Is there no one who will speak for me?"

Her eyes sought her husband Joacim, who was standing at the outer edge of the crowd in an attempt to be as inconspicuous as possible. He had apparently been unable to decide whether it would do less damage to his reputation to speak in her defence or to denounce her. Clearly, no timely help would be forthcoming from that source

Suddenly, Daniel stepped from the mass of onlookers. He was, at this formative stage of his career, still an ambitious young lawyer, and situations like this didn't surface every day. Wealthy, respected principals...prurient details...a beautiful defendant whose life was on the line... Daniel recognized the sensational potential of the case immediately and was not about to pass it up.

"I object to this travesty of justice," he announced dramatically. "Allow *me* to represent you, good woman!"

Susanna pondered for just a moment. She had hoped for someone with a little more clout. But she didn't see anyone more suitable springing eagerly to her defence. He was her only chance. Hiding her reservations from the onlookers, she accepted his advocacy.

"I'll need to talk to my client alone for a few minutes," he demanded.

"Fine. But stay where we can see you. She's in enough trouble already."

Oh, sure, thought Susanna...*like it could get worse.*

As they strolled along a well-tended path in full view of the assembly, Susanna rapidly murmured instructions, while Daniel nodded complacently. But when they returned she was the embodiment of modest humility.

Daniel faced the assembly.

"Are you actually going to accept the unexamined words of these two old reprobates without corroborating evidence?" he mocked. "At least allow me to examine them separately. Keep them apart. *Far* apart ...so they can't collaborate on their responses. Look at their crafty old faces. They can't be trusted."

This arrangement was accepted, and he addressed the first of the accusers. "You saw this woman commit adultery?"

"I did. I saw it all."

"Then you remember it vividly?"

"I'll never forget it. It was disgusting! I can tell you every detail..."

"Don't bother." There was a general murmur of disappointment. "Just tell us under which tree the evil deed was done."

"Which tree?"

"Yes. Which tree?"

"Well...they were under a small mastic tree."

"You're sure?"

"Absolutely. A mastic tree."

"How can you be so certain? You're not as young as you used to be. Perhaps your memory is failing."

"My memory is just fine...and we were so close we could almost smell the resin."

"You couldn't be mistaken?"

"Certainly not."

Daniel allowed a meaningful pause as he glowered at the witness. "God is going to get you for this!" he snapped. "Next!"

The old man was escorted away and his equally ancient crony was immediately called forward.

"And I suppose," Daniel started, "that your memory is quite as clear as that of your fellow?"

"I should hope so!"

"And you swore that the act of adultery took place in this very garden, I think."

"Absolutely."

"Then you can tell us where, precisely. Under which tree?"

"It was under the big old holm tree you can see stretching above the others over there."

"How can you be so sure you remember the exact tree?"

"Well, look at it...it's *huge*. Anyway, what possible difference does it make?"

The assembled crowd began to murmur, angrily.

"What difference?" shouted Daniel histrionically. "Merely this: it proves that you're a lying old reprobate —and so is your accomplice. And the angel of God is just waiting with a really sharp sword to cut the both of you from stem to sorry stern..." He was beginning to work himself up into a lather, when his glance fell on Susanna, who brought him back to the job at hand with a disapproving frown.

"In fact, you've tried this despicable gambit before, haven't you? The word around the women's quarters suggests that you have a nasty habit of threatening ladies who catch your eye with exactly this kind of bogus charge if they don't accept your miserable attentions. How many girls have been too scared to resist, you filthy worm? This fine lady," he turned to Susanna, who lowered her eyes chastely, "was simply too honourable to go along with your disgusting scheme."

And too clever, he thought to himself—much, much too clever.

The crowd, which had been cheated of the uplifting spectacle of a beautiful woman being put to death for her alleged sins, adjusted rather well to the last minute substitution of two wicked old men... for the law of Moses required that the same punishment be meted out to the bearers of false witness as they had intended for the innocent defendant. So a good time was had by all—except perhaps the two old sinners themselves. And even those two were at least spared the ordeal of facing their wives who, without a doubt, would have made them *wish* they were dead.

Susanna, of course, went home to her happy, happy family, where she spent the reminder of the day and the greater part of the night discussing quite frankly with Joacim the nature of the active and enthusiastic support which she had expected from him, and which, sadly, had been so very conspicuous by its absence.

And we most certainly can't forget Daniel, who considerately spared Susanna any further unwelcome public attention by taking full credit for her release onto his own willing shoulders and strutting away with it. His legal theatrics had placed him front and center among the Jews, which was exactly where he wanted to be, and nudged him another step closer to the environs of power.

Chapter 14

Gomer

In the days of the kings, when Hosea—who saw himself as one of God's moral watchdogs—felt called upon to take a wife, some perversity in his nature impelled him to seek out a soul he might save in the process.

After diligent and exhausting research among the whores available in the vicinity, he chose a vibrant young cultic prostitute named Gomer, whom he was able to acquire for the modest sum of fifteen pieces of silver and twenty-one bushels of barley at a temple liquidation sale. Marrying the girl without delay, he eagerly looked forward to reforming her, as a service to The Lord. The Lord, no doubt, was suitably grateful.

Gomer, unfortunately, was not. As a priestess in the service of the ancient Sumerian goddess Inanna, the plump, warm-hearted girl had taken great pride in her role of healer, easing the needy men who paid for her services. This pride, in fact, often translated itself into downright enthusiasm...which didn't make her any less popular among the lovelies on offer. Hosea's assumption that she was damaged, tainted goods in need of redemption found no reflection whatever in her self-image. She had been taught that the priestesses who worshipped the Great Goddess embarked on each sexual act as if it were fresh and quite untouched by all previous experiences... bearing no guilt, no shame. These dedicated ladies were virtual virgins—by profession.

It was on her wedding night that she first encountered in the attitude of her new husband the unfamiliar concept of virginity as a non-renewable resource—a possession to be purchased, owned, and used up in an instant of time.

"Have I offended you?" she asked. "You turn your head away."

"Take no notice," he groaned. "I must brace myself."

"Why, what's the matter?"

"Well...you must know!" He wrinkled his nose. "Your body has been *used*...by *others!*"

"Well," she laughed, "I suppose so. "But all the important bits are there, I assure you...and in excellent working order, I've been told. What does it matter?"

But she found that it *did* matter. Her enthusiasm for the married state waned as she found she was to be treated with condescending distaste by her pious husband—a distaste which did not, however, prevent Hosea from making effective use of the compromised body of his pagan bride, you can be sure.

Three babies were born to this badly matched couple, and Gomer lavished her love and joy on them while her devout husband continually struggled to bend her lively spirit to his own circumscribed perception of worship. Then, as the children grew older and seemed to need her devotion less, she turned to the attention of lovers for the affection she needed to keep her soul alive. She wasn't overly discreet, and her husband, always on the alert for infractions of every conceivable moral law, inevitably found her out.

Outraged, Hosea cursed her and banished her from the house, then spit out his rage at their unfortunate children. "Your mother is a whore," he screamed. "You'd better hope she mends her sluttish ways and gets back here...and soon...or I'll kick you *all* out into the street. You're nothing but spawn of a whore!

"You know...maybe I won't even *take* her back. Why should I take back twice-damaged goods? That would serve you *all* right. You'll starve...and it's no more than you deserve."

Strangely, the children showed no sign of offering him the warm, loving support and sympathy Hosea might have expected under the circumstances. They were terrified, and they wanted their mother.

While Hosea wallowed in lascivious images of his wife, draped in silks and jewels as a rich man's plaything, Gomer danced barefoot on sacred mountaintops. The lively girl had mourned for the mirth and the feast days, the new moons and the sabbaths of her former life while her self-righteous husband had stopped his ears and refused to understand. In his pinched perception, her joyous worship of the Goddess Inanna was one with the bloody cult of Baal, and his jealous god allowed him to think no further.

As time passed, though, he began to miss the light she had shed on the stifling circle of his life. The days seemed greyer without her and by the time he set out to search, he was wondering what he could say to lure her back.

He mentioned his dilemma to one of the less sanctimonious of his friends, over a parting cup of watered-down wine.

"Focus on the kids," advised his pal, between sips. "She must be missing the kids. That'll be your best bet."

"Of course!" replied Hosea. "She loves those kids a lot. She's got to be missing them something terrible. Lucky I didn't throw them out into the street yet...*that* would have been awkward! Thanks."

He found her, burning incense in the cool and leafy shadows of a sacred grove. Reluctantly she listened as he begged her to return.

"If it's nature you want," he observed, gazing about him with a puzzled air, "we'll move to the country. You can have as much nature as you like. You can have vineyards...freedom...fig trees...

"Think," he insisted. It would be a great place to bring up the kids—did I mention that they miss you? They cry...all the time. And..." he added, after a painfully visible struggle with his conscience, "you may even... sing...if you like. Sometimes."

The thought of her children brought tears to her eyes and melted her resolve. This did not go unnoticed by the watchful Hosea.

"Of course," he appended, "you must never, *ever* pray to your foul, vicious god again."

She looked sadly down at the flower-strewn altar. "Goddess," she whispered, "...you idiot."

For the sake of the children, she returned, and Hosea magnanimously forgave her. In fact, he forgave her with such remarkable fervour that he found he rather enjoyed it, so she had to hear him pointing out and forgiving her for each of her transgressions, large and small, year after year, to the end of her days. And he got quite good at it. As time passed, he became able to recognize and forgive sins she had never even *thought* of committing.

He had promised beauty and freedom and song. She got sour grape vines and continual judgment—for a lifetime.

Gomer never again spoke the name of the Great Goddess. She worshipped...nothing. And she certainly never sang. There seemed to be nothing much to sing about.

Chapter 15

Jonah

When it came to his attention one day that the city of Nineveh was misbehaving in some particularly objectionable way, The Lord sought a suitable representative to make his displeasure known to the inhabitants. He made every effort to select the best available candidate but all the really good people appeared to be otherwise occupied, so he chose Jonah instead. Jonah fell rather short of being the ideal delegate—he was lazy and cowardly, and his moral fibre was somewhat frayed in spots—but he had been to Nineveh before and he was definitely available, as he was out of work most of the time and this particular time was no exception.

"Jonah," called God, "I have a job for you."

"You're kidding," answered Jonah. "You sure you want me? There's a better guy down the road...I think his name is Jonas. Maybe you're looking for him."

"You've been to Nineveh?" asked The Lord.

"For a couple of years," said Jonah, "...a while ago."

"It's you I want. There's a lot of wickedness going on in Nineveh. I want you to go there and warn the people to cut it out."

"Um... well..." stammered Jonah. "I'm flattered... honestly! But...well...I'm pretty busy right now."

"No," snapped The Lord. "You're not. Now get going."

Something in God's tone suggested to Jonah that this might not be the most politic time to mention the pretty shop girl he had seduced on his last trip to Nineveh. On his reluctant way to the harbour, though, he had time enough to relive his uncomfortably narrow escape from the protective brothers who were determined to avenge her honour, and on his arrival at the dock, he promptly booked passage on the first available ship headed in exactly the opposite direction. Then, just in case God should think to check on him, he hid himself in a secluded cranny below deck and prepared to snooze his way to land.

Well, it's not so simple to deceive God. Many have tried...few have succeeded. And every one of those was much wilier than Jonah, even on their most inept days. He had barely gotten comfortable before The Lord noticed that he was headed in an unauthorized direction. Waiting until the ship got well out to sea, The Lord stirred up a nasty great wind and aimed it in Jonah's direction. As the impromptu tempest tossed the ship about in a most distressing manner, the mariners hastily attempted to contact their own heathen gods in order to find out what was the problem. Their gods, however, failed to respond as they had all been occupied elsewhere and knew nothing whatever about it.

As they searched about for loose goods to cast overboard in order to lighten the ship's burden, they happened across Jonah in his snug little hidey-hole and dragged him up onto the deck.

"Pitch him over the side, the little sneak," insisted one. "This is probably his doing!"

Jonah was beginning to feel decidedly unwelcome, surrounded as he was by a crowd of hostile seamen screaming at him over the crashing waves. The din drew the attention of a particularly surly-looking fellow who had been occupied in struggling with the sails. He bellowed in rage.

"I know him! He's a Hebrew, and he ruined my sister. The weasel defiled her then skipped town. What are you waiting for? Throw him overboard!"

They didn't wait to be asked twice. Over he went.

God's attention was spread a bit thin that day, and it was a few hours before he remembered to call off the storm. But the mariners were a tough lot; except for a few rope burns and a serious splinter, they all survived intact and were able to keep their sturdy ship afloat.

In the meantime, Jonah was having problems of his own. On leaving the ship, he plummeted like a rock, certain that he had breathed his last. But The Lord wasn't done with him yet. A vagrant whale, trolling for snacks in the turbulent waters beneath the vessel, swallowed him up and he found himself sloshing about in the creature's belly with a fairly disgusting smorgasbord of marine creature bits and pieces. His relief at being saved from drowning was tempered by the obvious discomforts of his lodgings, but he suspected that it might be unwise to complain right away, so he made himself as comfortable as possible and settled down to wait.

He waited for three long days and three equally tedious nights, picking the seaweed out of his hair and watching the skin on his fingertips shrivel from the wet. Finally, the stench of digestion was too much for him, and he ventured a prayer to the Almighty.

"I know it was you who saved me, Lord, and I can't thank you enough. I'm ready to leave now, if you have a moment to spare. I know I owe you a sacrifice already, but everything down here is way too repulsive...not suitable at all. Maybe later."

This seemed to satisfy God, for he inspired the whale to vomit Jonah up onto the land. The whale was more than delighted to comply, in fact. Jonah himself smelled none too fresh by now, and the creature had been having trouble keeping down his breakfast while this unpalatable guest was on board.

It should have been no surprise to Jonah to find that he had been deposited within walking distance of a large and suspiciously familiar-looking metropolis. There would be no backing out this time.

"Nineveh," insisted The Lord, who had stopped by just to make sure. "Now!"

As he trudged reluctantly toward the city, Jonah resigned himself to completing his assigned task, but he was determined to keep a low profile. With any luck at all, he thought, he could deliver his message and be gone before his jilted lover even suspected his presence. On entering the gates, he rushed straight to the city's centre, intending to mutter his warning to whichever stragglers were close enough to hear it and then scurry discreetly away.

His tight itinerary had not allowed him time to freshen up before addressing his audience. The heavy aroma of whale gut still hovering about him was enough to keep everyone at a considerable distance, so he was forced to shout out his carefully rehearsed message, if he was to be heard at all. He'd kept it as short as possible:

"Yet forty days, and Nineveh shall be overthrown!"

Only eight words, but bursting from the lips of a raggedy, odorous wretch with fish scales still clinging to his stringy hair... well, they must clearly be considered the utterances of one of God's true prophets! Gamely overcoming their initial aversion, the crowd surged toward Jonah, sweeping him to their shoulders where he bobbed like a particularly objectionable bit of flotsam.

"Repent! Repent, and God may relent!" they shouted, to no one in particular.

The king insisted on being kept informed of all such divinely-inspired threats of imminent destruction so that immediate preventative measures could be taken to save the city. On this occasion, he ordered strict fasting and sackcloth with a liberal topping of ashes, throughout the city. No exceptions.

Hungry, thirsty and dishevelled, the city awaited The Lord's reaction.

Fortunately, God was favourably impressed and more than a little flattered by this prompt and suitably obsequious response. He immediately cancelled the overthrow and the city was allowed to go on very much as it had before Jonah's arrival.

Once the disaster had been averted, Jonah's celebrity as prophet of the hour came to an abrupt end (crowds are fickle that way); not, however, without attracting the unwelcome attention of his former sweetheart. The temper of her burly band of brothers had not improved over the intervening years, and a few loose teeth and a broken head sufficed to convince Jonah that marriage would throw a desirable cloak of respectability over his former indiscretion.

Within a few days, he realized that his new wife was no longer the timid, biddable girl he had left behind. The marital balance of power wobbled in a most unsettling manner. He needed to put her in her place.

"Don't you think you'd better be getting back to work now?" he asked. "I'm surprised your boss hasn't come looking for you by now. The honeymoon's over, my girl...we're going to need money to live, you know."

"My boss?" she laughed. "Oh, no worries about that. You don't think I've spent all this time pining over *you,* do you? Small chance! I have a booth of my own in the marketplace now. I *am* the boss."

"Well, that *is* good news." Jonah lay back with a smug smile at this unexpected good fortune and began spinning fond dreams of a life of genteel leisure.

"But since you mention it," she said, "I do have some plans. I can't say I was ever looking forward to see *you* again, but since you're here, we may as well get started right away. The booth is doing so well that I'm opening a suburban branch in a promising district right outside the city precincts. I've been looking for someone to operate it for me, but you'll do just fine. You can start tomorrow."

"But I've never..."

"You'll learn. And it'll save us paying someone else."

"But..."

"Tomorrow. Early. I'll see that you're awake." Since she was now stuck with him, she intended to wrench some small value out of what had appeared to be a sadly unpromising union.

The job didn't suit Jonah at all. There weren't many customers yet so the duties were light, but he had to tend the goods for a significant proportion of each day, and the sun bouncing off the city wall built up a most unpleasant concentration of heat inside the little stall. To the delight of several agile thieves in their tireless search for free samples, Jonah was soon devoting all his attention to the cultivation of a gourd vine that would create a leafy bower overhead for his protection.

But perhaps God finally remembered Jonah's former shabby behaviour toward his paramour... something he had chosen to overlook in his eagerness to recruit a spokesman. Finding the culprit dozing comfortably in his shady retreat, The Lord dropped off a hungry worm to wither the gourd plant and a particularly arid and persistent wind to desiccate the sleeper. He intended to return with a more meaningful punishment sometime later, but other more pressing duties intervened, and it completely slipped his mind.

Jonah awoke, parched and sunburnt, and saw that his horticultural efforts had been mysteriously blighted while he snoozed. Not being an actively persistent sort of chap, he gave up on gardening— which was altogether too much like work anyway— and spent the remainder of his life whining about his discomfort and nagging at his busy wife to have a canopy constructed to shade his days. She always promised to look into the matter, but what with one thing and another, she never did get around to it.

It was probably just an oversight.

Chapter 16

Judith

Shortly after the return of the Jews from their extended visit to Babylon, the ruler of that powerful land was obsessed by a vague, nagging sense that he had been grievously disrespected in some indefinable manner, and he became determined to exact revenge on pretty much anyone he could find.

By the time his army, led by the valiant Holofernes, had reached Judea, the men had acquired quite a reputation for plundering temples, to say nothing of the usual wartime slaughter and destruction. The children of Israel had been prepared to tolerate with relatively good humour most of the traditional forms of devastation, but they had only recently rebuilt their own temple in Jerusalem and carted all their altars and sacred vessels and knick-knacks back from Babylon, and they weren't at all eager to have them snatched away again. So they secured their mountaintops, fortified the hill country villages, gathered in all available victuals, and dug in their heels.

"The mountain passes allowing access into Judea are very narrow," remarked the most influential of the Jewish elders. "We've got that much going for us. They would allow only two enemy soldiers to pass through abreast."

"Maybe three," suggested a slightly younger elder. He had an annoying habit of picking flaws.

"Maybe three... but they'd be tripping over each other's spears. The risk of a bottleneck would be tactically unsound."

" 'Tactically unsound'...listen to him...he's a general now! Pardon me, mister general."

"Oh, just post a few spare goatherds to watch for any sign of intruders, and don't be so sarcastic. We have more important issues to address: have the people been told to don their regulation sackcloth and ashes?"

"I don't know...I don't remember seeing the streets looking any dustier than usual this morning. My own outfit is, of course, ready for use at any moment..."

"Well, see that they're alerted... you know it's customary to resort to sackcloth and ashes when confronted with threats of this kind! Keep them busy praying and fasting...and if anyone cares to offer a few token gifts to their Creator...well, that might not be such a bad thing either. Let me see...sackcloth...ashes ...prayer...gifts...yes, I think that should about cover it."

Just in case, a few of the more enterprising of the fighting men and youths prepared to defend the passages by whatever means might seem expedient at the time—but only if the goatherds couldn't handle the job.

When Holofernes' soldiers arrived at the mountain passes, they found the heights manned by a handful of scruffy-looking goatherds, and a sprinkling of Jewish defenders armed with slingshots and an assortment of largish rocks. The battle-hardened Babylonian warriors had barely recovered from their initial burst of raucous laughter and settled down to invent suitably belittling taunts when the rocks and stones began to rain down on them, confined as they were, with remarkably deadly effect. The jeering smiles had faded from the lips of the survivors long before they reached Holofernes' headquarters with a sheepish report of their embarrassing little setback.

The Babylonian hero accepted their account with apparent insouciance. In fact, he hummed a sprightly little tune throughout, to indicate that he was barely listening at all. But when they were quite finished—and without admitting for one moment that his prized fighting force had been bested—Holofernes coolly ordered that the fountains providing water for nearby Bethulia be secured and held. He manned all nearby mountaintops to ensure that no one could leave the city...and waited patiently for the inhabitants to die of thirst.

It didn't take long. Within a couple of weeks, it was necessary for the city fathers to strictly limit the use of wash water, and those who had been most liberal in their application of ashes were beginning to regret their enthusiasm, as the grit worked its way through grimy garments to scalp and skin. When the city ran out of water completely, an insistent crowd of thirsty, unkempt and irritable people approached Ozias, who was a governor of the city, with a suggestion:

"We've been weighing the advantages of your present strategy—the one where we hold tight and die of thirst—and frankly, we can't see much in it. It's time to surrender."

Ozias could see that they had a point, but he wasn't ready to give up on divine intervention just yet. "Hang in there for five more days," he pleaded, with tears caking the ash on his cheeks. "If God doesn't send us something in the way of help by then, I promise to give up the city... and... " he sobbed a little, "precious Jerusalem will be doomed."

Recognizing that a five day delay would probably cost them little more than the lives of a few really old people and perhaps a couple of the very sickliest infants, the townsfolk reluctantly agreed, but not without a whole lot of grumbling.

Not *every* inhabitant was content to wait idly for The Lord to lend a hand. Judith had been widowed at an uncommonly young age and had grieved in the prescribed manner for over three years, fasting assiduously the whole time. It had not improved her rather spirited temper one bit. She demanded an interview with Ozias.

"We can't surrender!" she insisted. "We'll leave Jerusalem unprotected, and it's The Lord's most favourite city. He won't be pleased, and you know how moody he can get. I heard you're extending the order for ashes and prayers. Are you kidding? This is your siege response plan? How many times do you expect that old number to work, anyway?

"And another thing, she went on. "Was it your idea to give God a five day deadline to kick in with some help? You figure because you make an agreement, he has to drop everything and come running? Why don't we prime the pump a bit? He might be more inclined to make a special trip here to help us out if he sees we're doing some little thing to help ourselves—something besides wallowing in ashes and waiting to surrender."

Ozias chose to overlook the ever-so-slightly critical tone of her words. "But you see, my dear," he explained, "the people are getting thirsty...and they get testy when they're uncomfortable. They made me promise to surrender...and we can't break our oath, now, can we? ...So run along home to pray like the others, and maybe God will send us rain to fill our cisterns. *That* would spoil the enemy's little plan, wouldn't it?" He patted her hand in that condescending way old people sometimes have.

Judith stared at him coldly. "Well, prayer isn't enough! Somebody has to *do* something. And since it seems like you can never find a hero when you need one, I guess it'll have to be me."

On reaching home, she shrugged off her widows' weeds and the ubiquitous sackcloth, assiduously brushed the grime out of her hair, and braided it in a fetching style cleverly chosen to distract attention from any stubborn ashy residue. She rooted among the garments she'd worn when she was dating her late husband and donned her most alluring dress, completing the effect with perfume, precious ointments, an assortment of her most costly jewellery and a pair of strappy little sandals.

Summoning her faithful serving maid, she revealed the plan she had formulated on her way home. "I'll need your help. It's bold," she admitted. "It's risky. Are you with me?"

"Well, let me see..." replied the girl. "Die of thirst, surrender like a slave...or tackle an adventure. Hmmm. Whatever shall I choose? *Of course* I'm coming with you."

Together, they packed a particularly large bag with wine and oil, parched corn, fine bread and some juicy big lumps of figs, and set off out the city gates.

When they approached the enemy camp, they had no trouble at all attracting the attention of the posted lookouts—almost any seductively dressed female approaching from the mountains would have been able to do so.

Adjusting her manner to her audience, Judith spoke out boldly. "Hey, we've just escaped from Bethulia. The city is getting dirty...and it stinks. Do you know where we can get a hot bath? I know you weren't expecting guests, but I have information that could save you all a lot of trouble. If you'll take me to your chief, I'm sure we can work something out."

The soldiers had not failed to notice that she was beautiful. "I'm sure you can," admitted the ranking captain. They led her to Holofernes' tent.

Ignoring the grinning soldiers, Judith composed herself and stepped unannounced past the tent flap. The tent was furnished, for the most part, in the most utilitarian manner: weapons, maps and a sparse table with a single chair. But to one side lounged the great man himself, on a gorgeous bed draped in rich purple under an elaborate canopy encrusted with a gaudy assortment of sumptuous gems. Judith's lips turned up in an enigmatic smile. *This man,* she thought, *fancies himself, above all others. This man,* she thought, *is exactly who I expected him to be.*

Holofernes studied the woman before him, noting with satisfaction the pleased expression on her beautiful face. *She likes what she sees,* he thought smugly. He allowed himself to display a nobly condescending smile with subtly sensuous overtones, as she explained once more her flight from Bethulia.

"Well, you'll find that we Babylonians know how to treat beautiful women," he smirked.

"I see you're as gracious as you are mighty." Her words fairly dripped with flattery...and he loved it. "Even in a backwater like Bethulia, we've heard that the great Holofernes is the power behind the Babylonian throne. I didn't dare to hope that so great a warrior would be so chivalrous." She managed a becoming blush. "It is very...attractive," she murmured. *The great conceited oaf,* she thought. *He believes that every woman is as easy to impress as his camp-following doxies.*

"I've come here prepared to serve you...in whatever small way I can," she offered.

Holofernes moistened his lips in anticipation.

"It has been said that the Jews can't be conquered unless they sin against their God," she went on, her tone becoming distinctly businesslike. She paused a moment to enjoy his disappointment. He'd been expecting something more seductive. "Well, it's true.

"But the Bethulians are starving and their water is running out," she added. "Soon they'll start eating all sorts of food that their dietary laws forbid. When they get desperate enough to share the portion that's been reserved for the priests, God will have a fit!

"When that happens, He'll be too busy sulking to protect them. Lucky for you, I have a unique rapport with The Lord. Let me go out into the valley every night and pray. When the people have committed these sins, God is bound to come complaining to me. Then I'll tell you, and you can destroy the city with no problem at all.

"After that, I can lead you through Judea to Jerusalem. Once God is on your side, you should be able to conquer it without losing a man. Well, how does that sound?"

Holofernes imagined riding back in triumph to Babylonia as conqueror of Jerusalem and with his army intact.

"I suppose it's worth a try," he acceded.

His attention wandered once again to her tempting presence in his boudoir. "Comfortable accommodations will be arranged for you within the camp, but you may be my guest for dinner, if you like. I'm sure I can provide everything you might desire. Can I offer you anything?" he hinted, suggestively. "Anything at all?"

"As enticing as that sounds," answered Judith, "I must decline. We've brought our own food... those pesky dietary restrictions, remember?"

"So what happens when your provisions run out?' he asked.

"Oh, don't worry about that," she replied. "They won't run out before I'm done here."

So every midnight, Judith and her maid carried their food bag out past the guards, and picnicked beside a delightfully secluded fountain nearby. The big bag was gradually emptied of its provisions and the two women whispered together, perfecting their plans.

On the fourth day Holofernes summoned Judith to his tent. He was sure she fancied him— she had practically thrown herself at him, as he remembered. It would be positively *rude* to reject so available a gift.

"I'm planning a banquet this evening," he said. "Do you think you'll be free? It'll be quite small...intimate, really. A private affair..." he suggested, with a leer.

"Certainly," replied Judith, looking into his eyes. "Whatever pleases you." She sauntered back to her quarters and, with her maid's help, selected a casually enticing silk robe for the evening's festivities. A few frivolous pieces of jewellery and her most blatantly suggestive perfume completed the ensemble.

"All tarted up and ready to go," she quipped to her maid. "Wish me luck."

By the time she re-joined Holofernes, he was nearly shaking with passion, but he was determined to play it cool. It wouldn't do for a man of his stature and obvious charms to appear too eager.

"Try not to be intimidated," he drawled languidly. "I'm just like almost any other man. You must have a drink with me. I insist."

"Well," she started, "the dietary laws, you know. But tonight..." she simpered, "tonight I simply can't seem to help myself! I can't drink *this,* of course, but I've had my maid prepare wine especially for me. You won't be insulted, will you?"

Holofernes waved aside her concerns. "No, no. Not at all. I'm delighted...delighted!" He threw back a glass of his own potent favourite...and another. And with each drink, he felt more powerful and more desirable. In his eagerness to wring every last drop of pleasure from the encounter and impress this dainty tidbit with his virility, he soaked up enough wine to incapacitate an ox.

By late evening, he had collapsed, helplessly drunk, on the bed. All the waiters and servants had been dismissed in anticipation of a night of passion, so he and his guest were entirely alone. *Heaven knows,* thought Judith, *nothing could be allowed to mar the glamour of a romantic evening with an amorous drunk!*

Ever so quietly, she slipped Holofernes' sword from the bedpost where it hung obscenely, with its razor edge glinting in the candlelight. Grabbing a fistful of his hair in one hand, she swung the deadly weapon with the other. Blood spurted everywhere, and the head now dangled at a most unpleasant angle. *Damn,* she thought, *distasteful chores of this nature seem always to be so much more difficult than one might hope. A single blow would have been much neater.* She wished, fleetingly, that she'd had an opportunity to practice a bit, perhaps with a melon, or a gourd—this kind of thing was not at all in her line—but there just hadn't been time. She sawed away until the neck was completely severed and wrapped the head in the concealing folds of the silken bed canopy. *How lucky the vain fool didn't use mosquito netting, like any normal person.*

The merest whisper brought the maid, who had been patiently awaiting her cue outside the tent with an appropriate change of clothes and a light kosher snack. Together they stuffed the carcass under the bed with the bloodiest of the sheets—there was no sense drawing unnecessary attention to their evening's work. While Judith freshened up, the maid tucked the head, canopy and all, into their conveniently empty food bag and the two women were ready to saunter casually out of the camp as usual.

A couple of hours later, entry was demanded at the gates of Bethulia by two tired and impatient women carrying a rather heavy bag which appeared to be badly in need of laundering.

Despite the late hour, Judith was immediately questioned by the elders. "How'd it go?" asked Ozias.

"Not bad," answered Judith. "The Babylonian army isn't much of a threat without Holofernes. And *he* won't be causing us any more trouble."

"Are you sure?"

"It's in the bag."

"How can you be so certain?"

"No...really. Look in the bag."

They did. "Oh. Yes," they admitted. "That should do it. What's this jewelled rag?"

"It's the remains of his love nest. Just a practical joke...you can throw it away, if you like."

Ozias looked shocked. "I hope you didn't compromise your honour!"

"With that drunken lout? Certainly not."

"Thank God! We could never have lived with the shame."

A torchlight procession and public celebration was quickly organized, and Ozias mounted the podium to address Judith formally.

"See here the head of Holofernes," he intoned. "The Lord has smitten him by the hand of a woman! Blessed are you and blessed is the God who directed you to destroy this evil man."

To tell the truth, Judith wasn't so sure *what* God might think of her deed, but eliminating Holofernes had seemed to be the most effective available option at the time. If she could have thought of something tidier ...well, that would most certainly have been her first choice.

Judith accepted the tribute in silence then took the opportunity to offer a suggestion: "You might want to think about hanging that head from the battlements. It's a bit of a mess, but the morning sun should highlight the most recognizable bits. With any luck, the Babylonians will take the hint and move on. It's the best chance you're likely to have to get rid of them without any significant risk to yourselves."

Holofernes' head was displayed artistically on the city wall, and everyone went home to bed. Sure enough, as soon as the morning sun lit the severed head, the enemy suspected that something might be amiss. The bloody face looked disturbingly familiar, and a closer investigation of Holofernes' tent revealed the leftover torso, stashed under the bed. A quick check of Judith's empty tent confirmed the unthinkable: the great general had been brutally murdered, right under their noses—by a woman—and she had gotten clean away.

As the Babylonian troops milled around, leaderless and quite incapable of coordinating their next move, a conjecture began to circulate: *If the Jewish women are capable of such courage and resolve, what must be the ferocity of their men?* Without waiting for consensus on the answer, they promptly abandoned the camp and sprinted toward Babylon. The broad backs of the enemy troops presented excellent targets, and before long, the Bethulians had chased down and killed enough of them to make a return match unlikely.

The division of the spoils proceeded with only one small hitch. Agreement had been reached and distribution was about to proceed when the youngest of the generals noticed a troubling oversight.

"Um...aren't we forgetting something?" he ventured, reluctantly.

The others scowled at him. Newly promoted leaders could be so unnecessarily conscientious.

"I don't think so!" snapped the delegated paymaster. "What's your problem?"

"Well...I could be wrong, but...aren't we obliged to set aside Holofernes' personal effects for his conqueror?"

A stunned silence fell over the group.

"But...she's a woman!"

"Strictly speaking...I don't think that matters."

"But...Holofernes' things...that's some of the very best stuff!"

Portions were reluctantly recalculated and the loot was presented to Judith with much pomp and ceremony— all of it: tent, plate, bed, vessels... the lot. *Souvenirs of a fun evening*, she thought, scornfully. *Thanks a lot.*

She dedicated the whole lot to the temple. She didn't need it, she didn't want it, and she wouldn't accept it from the hands of the mighty warriors who had been too timid to wrest it from him themselves.

Judith's fame as the saviour of Jerusalem spread, but many of the most ambitious wife-seekers in Israel found themselves able to overlook that drawback in view of her considerable wealth. Nevertheless, she never remarried. Everyone agreed that she set the bar way too high, refusing to consider any man she couldn't respect. In consequence, she lived single and independent for the rest of her long, long life.

Naturally, she didn't overlook the maid who had so loyally followed her into danger. She freed her immediately and the two women continued to be the closest of friends, but they never reminisced about that awful night in Holofernes' tent. It had simply been something disgusting that had to be done, not unlike lancing a boil or cleaning up dog vomit.

While Judith lived and, indeed, for a long time thereafter, no enemy dared to threaten the Israelites. Of course, it may have been their fear of the fearsome Jewish fighting men that kept them away.

Chapter 17

Threats and Promises

Throughout the ancient times, the Jews endured their share of privations, but the one thing they were granted in abundance was prophets. Big ones, small ones, loud ones and whiney ones—there was never a shortage of prophets to nudge the Israelites back onto God's 'A' list when they went astray or to re-enlist them into God's service when enrolment appeared to be falling off.

The zeal of these enthusiastic men had a tendency to thrust them into the unfortunate role of wet blanket. It was a hazard of the trade.

When King Hezekiah pulled down the pagan altars and spiffed up the temple, improving the facilities for offerings and sacrifices to The Lord, the prophet Isaiah was quick to assure him that God no longer fancied charred meat and blood.

"There won't be much call for that kind of thing any more," he informed the king. "He's had his fill, and the whole ritual thing has become a bore. It was bound to happen, sooner or later. Bad luck." Quite naturally, Hezekiah was disappointed. He'd gone to a lot of trouble and had been hoping for some small show of appreciation.

As it happened, The Lord subsequently changed his mind, so it wasn't a complete waste. But nobody loves a spoil sport, and Hezekiah was never really able to warm up to the prophet after that.

Isaiah's next scoop was the announcement that the God of Israel had decided it was time to diversify. "He will now become the God of *many* nations," the prophet declared, enthusiastically. "Wars will cease and weapons will be re-forged into tools... you'll see. All the nations on the world will worship the One God, and He'll kick the ass of anybody who doesn't!"

The Jews were understandably ambivalent about this. It appeared that they would henceforth have to compete for God's attention with everybody else, and they had rather enjoyed knowing that they had the inside track. But they needn't have worried. It wasn't one of Isaiah's most stunningly successful prophesies.

While Isaiah undoubtedly had many sterling qualities, a sympathetic appreciation of women's lighter attributes was definitely not among them. His warnings that The Lord would personally drop by to punish them for their foibles had a hysterically shrill tone. "He'll trash your flashy clothes," the prophet screeched. "He'll bald your fancy hairdos and confiscate every piece of your jewellery, right down to the last frivolous toe ring." Indeed, his wishful thinking sank so low, at times, as to include the divine infliction of objectionable body odour and a selection of unpleasant genital diseases on the vain offenders. Although he confidently imagined that God was on his side in this matter, The Lord often had more important issues to address than the vanity of a few women with too much time and money on their hands. So while there were undoubtedly many women whose natural scent was unlike that of any known flower, others who contracted uncomfortable venereal diseases, and yet more who went unaccountably bald, very few had their personal adornments snatched away by the direct hand of God, and those few may not have been the particular ones Isaiah had in mind.

It would be natural to suppose that his desire for women had been entirely destroyed by his distaste for all things feminine. But as he roamed the land, conscientiously searching out vain women in order to report their sartorial transgressions to The Lord, Isaiah's eye fell on a prophetess who was much more to his taste. (We can only assume that she draped herself in unadorned sackcloth and neglected her hair altogether.) An unaccustomed and very physical passion rose up in him, and before it could be quelled by any stray whiff of perfume or strand of natural curl, he trailed her to her lodgings and beat upon the door, proposing in the most perfunctory terms to honour her with his holy seed. Because her thoughts flowed in a more heavenly direction—and because she found him unattractive in so many ways—the woman respectfully declined his generous offer, insisting that he leave the premises immediately and take his precious seed with him.

Fortunately, he'd had the foresight to bring along two of his most devoted followers to record the glorious occasion for posterity. When their powers of persuasion seemed unlikely to sway her, their four strong arms were usefully employed restraining the screaming, thrashing maiden as the irritated prophet hurried to impregnate her before the mood was completely spoiled.

Isaiah was leaving—in fact, he was half way down the block—when he remembered that he and he alone had the power to cleanse this woman of the terrible sin of fornication. Feeling ever so righteous, he reluctantly returned to offer her the precious boon of marriage.

"Are you decent, yet?" he ventured, peering around the door jamb. "I find that I cannot leave without putting this right." A damp linen rag narrowly missed his right ear. Despite her distraught condition, the dishevelled victim appeared to have excellent co-ordination

"You don't understand," he explained rather testily, keeping well to the left of the doorway and out of missile range. "I feel it is my sacred duty, at whatever cost to my own delicate sensitivities, to wipe away your sin and make a decent woman of you. Of course, it will be most inconvenient...I have several other pressing commitments...but I am prepared to marry you immediately...allowing you, of course a decent period for prayer and repentance."

Sadly, the prophetess' views on the value and sanctity of his suggestion varied dramatically from his own. The differences were quite irreconcilable. She turned him down indignantly and definitely and in the most colourful language, and Isaiah was forced to beat a hasty and most ignominious retreat, dodging the barrage of domestic utensils which she fired after him by way of emphasis.

Shortly after this incident, Isaiah diversified his offerings by branching off into a line of political prophesies. Among his visions for the future he included a nice image of the land of Judah being subjugated by the Assyrians, who would amuse themselves by herding the Jews together and shaving

their heads, their beards and even their feet. (Men's feet must have been a lot hairier in those days.)

So that the Jews wouldn't feel unfairly singled out by this humiliation, Isaiah predicted that the Egyptian and Ethiopian prisoners would be led away naked of buttock and barefoot, effectively deflecting the derisive comments of the Assyrian soldiers from the shorn children of Israel.

God must have considered that Isaiah was enjoying this part of the prophesy entirely too much.

"You think that's funny?" he asked the prophet.

"Well...a little funny," admitted Isaiah.

God reflected.

"I think I'll have you drop the sackcloth from your own skinny loins for a while. Yes...you do that! I want *you* to walk the land butt-naked and barefoot for three years. Next time maybe you'll think twice before wishing it on somebody else. Consider it Sensitivity Training."

As the naked prophet trudged along to the next town on his agenda, a pregnant seeress was seen pushing her way to the front of the delighted crowd that gathered to point and jeer.

Undeterred by the embarrassing price Isaiah had paid for his foray into political prophesy, the prophet Jeremiah warned the children of Israel that God was displeased with them. Again. Their captivity in Babylon was inevitable. He encouraged them to sit tight and make themselves at home there, assuring them that The Lord would bring them back to Israel after seventy years.

God was ambivalent.

"Why are you mixing in?" He asked.

"I'm just trying to cheer them up," answered Jeremiah.

"Who asked you to?" demanded The Lord.

"I thought it would give them some comfort, maybe."

"Well, it is a soothing, optimistic sort of prophesy," admitted The Lord. "But I like to keep people guessing."

"Sorry."

"No harm done. But I want you to warn them to pay no heed at all to prophets, because I'm not sending any out these days. They're getting out of control. Heaven only knows what they'll take it into their heads to prophesy next."

"I have to *tell* them that?"

"Definitely."

"But...that would mean *me."*

"It would, wouldn't it?"

"You're not making my job any easier."

"Tough."

Jeremiah's advice to trip willingly into captivity had been badly received by the rulers of Israel. It did nothing to raise the morale of the Jewish soldiers, and people in high places began to suspect him of collaborating with the Babylonians in order to generate some extra cash on the side. (This was long before mass communication made religious zealotry a lucrative career choice.) He was eventually taken prisoner and lowered by a frayed rope into a pit so full of mire that he sunk in it up to his waist. He tried to derive comfort from the thought that this was about as bad as it could get. And so it seemed, until a famine struck the city. The welfare of inconvenient prophets was not a priority on anyone's list, and Jeremiah was immediately forgotten altogether.

The king, who didn't have the worry of impending starvation to distract him, finally remembered the irritating prophet. He called his chief information officer to his side.

"Whatever happened to that pesky prophet?" he asked. "I think his name was Jeremiah."

"Oh, we found a place for him in that old sunken dungeon...you know, the one that keeps filling with mud. He's been a bit quieter there, I think."

"How is he?"

"Well, I don't know. The last report is dated a few days ago. We're short handed, you know."

"Has he been fed?"

"Oh, I doubt it. We haven't a lot of food to spare right now."

"Look, you'd better send somebody down there to get him out before he starves to death. I know he's a pain, but in case he really is a bona fide prophet...well, we don't need The Lord's ill will just now, on top of everything else, do we?"

A couple of spare kitchen servants were sent to pull Jeremiah out and hose him off. He looked so pathetic that the king allotted him a corner in the palace, where he spent most of his time giving everyone who would listen unwanted advice which they had no intention of following.

When the Babylonians conquered Jerusalem, the Babylonian general summoned his chief foreign administrator. "Didn't we find some sorcerer or magician or other stashed in one of the palace pantries," he asked, "...or maybe it was a latrine...?"

"He was a prophet, I think," corrected the officious bureaucrat. "...and he was in a largish sort of broom closet."

"Whatever. What's to be done with him?"

"I've spoken to the under-secretary in charge of seers and other subversives, and I understand that he's harmless. Anything he's likely to say will do us no harm, and might easily work to our advantage. Perhaps we should just turn him loose. In fact, in view of the demoralizing influence he's had on the Jewish fighting force, that seems the least we can do to show our appreciation."

The parade of prophets went on and on... haranguing, wailing, beseeching and condemning. There were poet prophets and herdsman prophets and one slightly dotty prophet who mistook a horde of locusts for an army of teeny tiny soldiers on teeny tiny steeds, sent on purpose to punish drunkards by destroying the grape crop.

There was even one prophet—his name was Habakkuk—who actually asked God a quite sensible question: Why punish the righteous while the wicked prosper? In an attempt to give an equally sensible answer, The Lord clarified the difference between righteousness and self-righteousness and pointed out people's overwhelming preference for practicing the latter. When it came to distributing rewards, God assured the prophet, *he* knew the difference...and he couldn't be deceived.

Of course, the people completely ignored such answers as didn't suit them, and pretended that the questions had never been answered at all.

Through the voice of prophet after prophet, The Lord persistently pounded away at one theme that could be neither misunderstood nor overlooked: *Love me,* he said. *Love me and no one else; fear me so that you will always obey me...always and unquestioningly.* He did not require understanding. He didn't want it. He wouldn't have it.

The least hint of disobedience was and would ever be punished with fire, famine, plague and destruction. There was no mistaking the message: *Worship me...or I'll hurt you until you do!*

But all the recorded prophets shared a single drawback. All of their voices were harsh, masculine voices, and the messages conveyed had the limitations of a man's perspective and were imparted in a language of demands and threats. A female prophet might have comprehended a subtler, finer textured message. Were there, then, no women among the prophets?

Of course there were...but their softer voices were edited out of the record long ago by people who found it more comfortable to obey than to understand.

###

Other Books by This Author

Dodging Shells
by W. L. Bertsch

An irrepressible young Canadian soldier, fighting his way through Italy in World War II has to make his own fun, but war is not for sissies, so it's not easy.

People are shooting at him…and they're not always missing!

Website http://wendybertsch.com